MARIA ANDREAS

I Tell You
Never Give Up

English Edition

Translated from French
by Jacqueline Tobin

*Unsuitable for those under 16
due to explicit content.*

Acknowledgments

Thank you to Peter Davies for the cover design and to Jacqueline Tobin (www.hugejam.com) for the formatting and for her translation that admirably captures the intimate heart of this modern tale!

PART ONE

TEARING
APART

1. Zoomy

Zoomy pulls on his dick, his eyes fixed on the small screen.

A hard porn movie lent him by his friend Jimmy. Tension too brief...

Explosion!

On the screen the girl continues her loud moans, writhing. And the guy straddles her, as if the tension goes on ... and on ... and on ...

With a proper man's cock and a delayed explosion, surpassing all ecstasy.

Zoomy himself, has already finished ...

He only feels the fresh spermatozoa that burst out onto his stomach. He closes his computer, gets up, wipes the sperm with his T-shirt and takes a piss. Then he lights a fag, takes a beer from the fridge, adds vodka and rips open a big packet of crisps...

He swallows a second, then a third:

"And those new ice creams his mother bought? With whole pistachios?" He scoffs four of them. He's a bit nauseated and remembers that his father has an awesome liqueur, to help with digesting it all. He lights up again, goes to the living room, takes the elixir from the cabinet and pours himself a big glass.

Above the drinks cabinet, he sees the photo his father took of two swans. His mother loves swans because they stay together all their lives…

In actual fact, Zoomy has never looked at this picture...

Those two long necks with perfect curves, dancing and embracing in a graceful kiss.

"All their lives?" chuckles Zoomy, lighting up another fag.

He drinks another glass and goes back to bed.

"I'd better stuff myself with Viagra like Paolo, otherwise I won't be able to guarantee Saturday!"

His iPhone flashes. It's a text from Paulo:

"What are you doing mate?"

"I'm eating and jerking off! You?"

"Fuck, what is this mess? We were waiting for you at Jimmy's for a lads' night out and weed?"

"I know…

I met a girl and … we had a drink at Gingko's."

"Did you at least get to fuck her?"

"No… "

"Total prick! See you tomorrow!"

Zoomy stubs out his cigarette and gets up to get a beer.

He burps. He makes an effort to burp loudly. Then he

puts on his headphones and ends up falling asleep...

…

"Johnny, it's time!"

He drags his bare feet in the kitchen. His eyelids are sticking together. There is a sickening taste in his mouth.

"You look tired son, don't you feel well?"

"Yes Mum, don't worry!"

"Your coffee and sandwiches! Hurry up, you're late!"

"I'm not hungry!"

"At least take a banana with you! You'll be hungry by midday!"

"Mum, is it okay if I spend my holidays in Spain with my mates? Paolo's aunt has a huge villa with a pool!"

"I discussed it with your father, and it's okay! If you pass your exams, of course!"

"Cool! See you tonight!"

"Wait, tonight? You're not going running with your father and your little brother?"

"Too much like hard work … and races aren't my thing!"

He's late. He runs to catch his bus. He enters, out of breath.

"Mate, have you burst your lungs or something? Have a fag! It was a hot evening, yesterday... "

Zoomy doesn't answer. He's smoking…

He thinks about Tatiana:

He spent two hours with her at Gingko's and he doesn't even know, if she has a nice ass.

"I didn't even look!" He kicks himself.

...

After class, he finds her at Maccy D's.

"Hi, can I sit down?"

He doesn't wait for the answer and puts his triple cheeseburger down opposite her. Tatiana is eating salad and drinking orange juice.

"Don't you feel hungry with this stuff?"

"No, I feel full of energy."

Tatiana is at the nursing school. Her mother worked as a nurse.

"Why worked?

Is she doing something else now?"

"She's dead!"

"Oh, sorry, I didn't know!"

"You couldn't guess. I never talk about it..."

"Your father, how's he?"

"He started to see a psyc... "

"Con artist!" Zoomy interrupts.

"Not at all! She helps him a lot. Not only with his mourning for Mum...

I have to go now, see you later!"

She gets up to return her tray and Zoomy sees that she has a run-of-the-mill ass... He rushes through his cheeseburger and beer, then goes to get an ice cream, which he races through, before returning to class...

...

"In 1944, Japanese suicide bombers had become living bombs, sacrificing themselves for the emperor and their country's honour!" The teacher explains.

Zoomy is still thinking about Tatiana.

Her mother was Japanese. Her father, on a business trip, had got her mother pregnant while she was studying medicine in Tokyo. So the two lovers had returned to this provincial town. After Tatiana's birth, her mother had resumed her nursing studies. She was working in the hospital, before being hit by a drunk driver in the morning. She had just finished her night on call ...

"All their lives!" Zoomy remembered wistfully ...

...

"All okay for the strip poker on Saturday, geezer? We invited the Blowjob Queen and Jimmy has stocked up on weed and beer. Bring all the food you can! This will be a total orgy mate, you'll love it!"

Paolo laughs. An overgrown kid's laugh. Explosive laughter.

Zoomy loves that laugh and he loves Paolo.

"The Blowjob Queen gave me head yesterday... paradise dude! You will so rate her... See you tomorrow!"

Zoomy crosses the big park, without rushing...

Spring is gently sliding in, affirming itself. The snow has melted and the ground is beginning to tremble. The ground whispers, the ground hums... Already the blackbirds are searching the sodden ground, looking for worms.

Zoomy pauses a while and closes his eyes…

He lights a fag. He still has to write his essay for tomorrow. He has no idea for it.

Nothing.

He feels empty...

...

"I never know what to write!" He confides to Tatiana.

"Zoomy, dig deep within yourself, your memories, your dreams! Do you have dreams, Zoomy?"

Zoomy doesn't answer. He wonders what keeps pushing him to sit down in front of this girl, who always has an answer for everything!

Tatiana smiles. Her eyes, delicately lashed, crinkle. She has a sweet and gentle face.

"Me, I dream all the time!"

"What do you dream about?"

"About a realm of transparency... "

"You're really weird! Do you…

Do you smoke weed?"

"No! You know, in my line of work, I see so many horrors due to drugs!"

"But weed... it's nothing!"

Tatiana looks out of the window:

"I come across so much suffering, so I'm a little obsessed with prevention!"

"Prevention?"

"Yes… I swim, I run, I go rock climbing."

"And if you've worked up a sweat after all of that, you still pig-out on ice cream?"

"I love it! But I love fruit salad too! With Mum we made delicious ones! I drink a lot of water, especially when I run!

But good wine too!"

She laughs,

"... and champagne!"

Zoomy looks at her dubiously...

"I love giant king prawns and, of course, fish, like in Japan"

"Do you ever do stuff that's shit?"

"Never! Never! I love life, rivers, birds, mountains...

My friends... "

"Do you consider a waste of humanity like me your friend?"

"Yes, Zoomy! And...

you're not a waste!"

She bursts out laughing.

"At least... not yet!"

...

When he found the park, to go to Jimmy's, Zoomy saw dozens of snowdrops under a tree. So white. So fresh. So pure...

Moved by so much fragility, he was annoyed at his emotion and lit a fag...

...

An evening full of laughter... of wriggling about!

An evening of a thousand and one nights!

What a kick it was, being given head by the Blowjob Queen, with a joint in one hand and a beer in the other!

Ah, yes... he sure as hell rated that!

...

On Sunday he met up with Tatiana again for a stroll along the river:

"I'm stupid!" he thought, "I don't like walking! At least we won't run, I managed to avoid that!"

"We're not running Zoomy, but we're breathing! Do you feel like the air is vitalised?"

"From 'Red Bull'?" hazarded Zoomy in reply, but regretted it straightaway.

Tatiana was not the type to give up.

"This air will purify the poison from your cigarettes!"

She inflated her lungs:

"I breathe every morning, ten minutes before getting up. I'm always in the best mood!"

"I prefer sin![1]" Zoomy thought to himself...

"Do you know what sin is?"

Tatiana stepped forward:

"Do you see my back?"

Instead, Zoomy was looking at her buttocks:

"Yeah... so?"

"So...

That's what sin is:

Turning your back on life... "

...

"Turning your back on life!" Zoomy hammered out rhythmically while masturbating...

_____

[1] This is a pun in the original, between 'j'ai la *pêche*' [in the mood] and le *péché* [sin]

But this time, without the moaning girl.

…

2. The Name

Fuck! You're not going to fall in love with a virgin maiden who washes asses rather than licks them? I swear, that sucks!"

"Paolo, it's...

I don't know. I'm good with her, I can tell her everything!"

"Right then mate, tell her why you're nicknamed Zoomy!"

Lowering the decibels of his laughter:

"You'll see, if she loves that?"

…

"My real name's John!"

"And Zoomy? Where do you get that from?"

Zoomy hesitated, he cursed himself:

"The guys... they nicknamed me that because I..."

He spat the rest out at top speed.

"I have a small dick that needs zooming in on!

Zooming... Zoomy!"

Tatiana was seized by enormous laughter.

"Frankly you guys, you're complicated! Complicated. And complex! It's mental!"

Zoomy is relieved:

He laughs too. He feels good...

Before parting, her starry smile whispered to him:

"Me, I'll call you John!"

…

He passed his exams.

Tatiana went to the Swiss Alps with her father.

Zoomy flew to Spain, with the lads.

Spain:

Paella and ice cream snacks.

Sun.

Sweat.

Sangria.

Sucking off…

Three weeks of lust, tension and explosions!

Three weeks of drunkenness...

Here and there, messages from Tatiana:

Ridiculous pictures, where she appeared decked out in a pink hat, like an old Japanese tourist.

"Sublime, the mountains! You sweat, you suffer, but you keep going. When you reach the top, nothing is more grandiose! The Alps embrace the clouds ...

Make love with the clouds..."

"Clouds make love?" stammers Zoomy drunkenly...

naked under the blazing sun.

"Make… love?"

...

On his return, his parents and his little brother were still in Italy.

The apartment seemed sad to him. Lifeless…

"Are you going to see your grandfather at the home for his birthday on Saturday?"

"Ok Mum! How's the holiday?"

"Wonderful Johnny, wonderful! Norbert swims like a champ now! And was yours good?"

"Super… See you later!"

...

On Saturday, he kept his promise:

Instead of the evening at Jimmy's, with this new drug that promised heights far higher than the Swiss Alps, he went to the home with a box of chocolates. He wasn't annoyed about it. He loved his grandfather.

"My Johnny, my own little Johnny!"

The old giant was sitting, nailed down. Unable to get up. But his beaming eyes kissed Johnny with the tenderness of eternity:

"Do you remember when we left in the early morning and found mushrooms before everyone else?" With a mischievous and sparkling smile: "And that we came back exhausted at nightfall?"

"It was awesome!" Johnny added. "Each time, they were blown away at the sight of our backpacks, stuffed to bursting point!"

"You haven't forgotten, have you Johnny, that I taught you to love flowers, trees, birds as if they were your friends?"

Johnny knelt at the old man's feet. He put his hands in his:

Moved…

Three hours of memories, laughter, questions. Questions with or without answers…

When Johnny got up, he ached everywhere.

"Do you still know the prayer I taught you, Johnny?"

Johnny loved his grandfather too much to lie to him.

"No, Grandpa... You know, we don't do that anymore these days."

"But me, my Johnny, I pray for you every day!"

He smiled:

"And at night too, when I can't sleep! I love you my Johnny, you are a good kid! "

…

"A good kid who's about to jerk off with a gross, x-rated movie!" Johnny thought on his way home. He wondered how the old giant, condemned to immobility, managed to light up with so much life, joy and love …

…

3. Jimmy

The next day, he was woken by the ringing of his iPhone:

It was Paolo.

"Are you stupid or what mate, six o' clock on a Sunday? I'm sleeping!"

"Jimmy's dead!"

"What? Are you kidding?"

"No, I assure you, it's bad shit!"

Paolo was crying. Zoomy realized it wasn't a game:

"I'm coming," he said, getting up.

He crossed the park as if in a nightmare. The snowdrops still had their heads bent. Asleep… "It was dodgy gear that bitch bought on the beach! Bad shit! We thought he was tripping… that he was… spaced-out, you know? And then… he wasn't moving anymore. Not at all! The Blowjob Queen called the ambulance… "

"Where is he now?"

"At the hospital morgue. His parents are coming back tonight!"

…

It all happened very quickly:

The haggard friends, the Blowjob Queen in black and in tears, Jimmy's mother twisted in an endless moan.

The coffin sliding away languorously.

Welcomed by the flames…

…

For the first time in his life, Zoomy knew suffering.

The real thing.

The one that sticks in the throat. That night and day dribbles out an acrid taste and an unbearable stench:

The stench of the soul…

…

It was an immense solace when he found himself alongside the river with Tatiana. They walked silently. Very close to each other, they sat down on a bench…

The majestic river sauntered. A blackbird whistled, another answered it from a nearby tree. The ducks slid lasciviously along the banks. In the distance, a pair of swans approached with their family… The parents supervised the three youngsters with a responsible fervency, in harmony with nature.

Zoomy thought of his mother…

Suddenly he could cry:

Could cry at last tears of fury!

He didn't understand how these ridiculous words escaped

him:

"Anyway, I jerk off to fucking porn movies!"

"Masturbation isn't abnormal for a teen, you know!"

"With Jimmy, we had a great collection! Even violent ones!"

"Personally, I reckon pornography cheats, with bodies transformed into machines!"

She moved her arms up to her chest, as if to protect herself:

"With horror movies, I'm scared! When Mum died, I binge watched them and almost didn't get over it!"

Zoomy began to cry again:

"Jimmy was a real friend! If you only knew, how we both laughed!"

Tatiana stood up:

"Come! I'll show you something."

He followed her, docile. Either way, he had no choice. He couldn't bear to remain tortured by his thoughts. They reached the forest and took a path bordered by brambles, which went up the hill. Already, you could tell that the autumn was getting impatient. The leaves were starting to flirt with amber and bronze. The grass had lost its freshness, but it was good, to feel it crunch underfoot. They arrived in front of a cave, in which Zoomy saw a statue of the Virgin Mary. And small night lights, lit at the statue's feet.

"You aren't a Bible-basher are you?" he worried.

"No John, I'm not even a believer!" But when Mum died, when I wanted to die too, I came here every day, to light a night light. It calmed me a lot."

They lit a night light for Jimmy...

Upon leaving, Tatiana took his hand and they walked back down without speaking, but as partners…

…

4. Gab

The next day, Zoomy went to the forest cave alone. It was mild. There were golden reflections in the sky. It was magical…

Zoomy decided to climb a little more. Then he sat down under a huge oak tree. He groaned, torn apart in the depths of that burning, that wandering...

Suddenly, he heard a rustle of leaves:

He noticed a squirrel, jumping like crazy in the neighbouring trees. It danced, it waltzed, it whirled about. It was almost flying from one tree to another! With an elegance and grace that was as harmonious as it was agile…

Zoomy felt a smile of wonder on his lips:

Such acrobatics! Such balancing! Such bewitching vivacity!

The squirrel descended along a trunk. Zoomy held his breath. It was approaching him... What splendour:

Those two eyes so alive. That tail, like a bouquet of angels' feathers. Those hands, with those miniscule fingers, that even so gripped tightly to what they grasped.

The squirrel, far from being fierce, looked at Zoomy with mischief in its eyes:

"Hello, my name is Gab!"

Zoomy barely jumped. Everything was so natural. So wonderful. So true…

"I'm John, or Johnny!" He didn't hesitate for a second, and was amused that he didn't say "Zoomy!"

"I know…"

Then the squirrel was silent. He watched him with his adorable little whiskered-nose, and eyes more human, than all the eyes Zoomy had encountered…

It was Zoomy who picked the conversation up again.

"Are you happy?"

"You know Johnny, me, I'm stuck within the law.

I fight to get my food, I fight against the cold, I make hiding places, reserves…

By the way, you wouldn't have some nuts to give me?"

Zoomy pulled out his chocolate bar and began to extract the hazelnuts, one after the other. Gab feasted. He was laughing with pleasure:

"I'm a big foodie!"

Then he became serious again:

"You Johnny, you are free! Do you know the very least? You, you can make choices!"

"You don't say! Choose what?"

"Choose to listen to **Mike… or Beelzeb!**"

"Mike or Beelzeb? I don't know them!"

"But they know you...

They know you better than you know yourself!"

"You're being mysterious?"

Gab continued, sitting on his back legs:

"Mike is radiant! Powerful! So powerful...

But he very rarely shows his power. Mike respects you more than anything in the world! He loves your freedom. He tries to protect it! And he's doing everything he can, to protect you, too!"

He laughed.

"Not very easy, with all the stupid stuff you get up to!"

Gab began to dance. Spreading his pretty little arms, and juggling his tail, with spellbinding virtuosity. Then he began to hum:

"Mike... is LIFE!"

"I have a best friend who just died!"

"I know, victim of Beelzeb! Don't worry about him! Keep sending him your loving thoughts and good energies!"

"That bad gear that got bought on the beach, was that Beelzeb?"

Gab was silent for a long time...

"Beelzeb is the one who hates beauty.

Who hates communion.

Who hates transparency.

He's the one that draws men into all forms of solitude, self-centered pleasures...

Speaking of pleasure, another hazelnut, please?"

He caught two and began to hop about:

"Gab is greedy, Gab is nice... Gab is beautiful!"

"And me, what am I to do? How do I choose?"

"Look, you need two things:

First a place of your own. That you like. Even just a corner!

It could be here, or in your room, or by the river. It doesn't matter: it will be your cave!"

He straightened up suddenly, intrigued:

"Oh look over there in the pine tree, the big black one is strutting his stuff in front of a female! Females adore him with his jet-black coat. Me, I think mine is prettier, with its fiery stripes! Don't you think so?"

"Yes, of course, yes, yes ... but my cave?"

"Your cave ...

Finding your cave is, in fact, the easy part. It's after that it gets complicated! You have to go down to the other cave... "

"Which one?"

"The one in your cor![2]"

"Cor, cor... what?"

"It's Latin, you doughnut!"

Gab began to dance again:

"Gab is pretty, Gab is a foodie and... Gab is a scholar! A hazelnut and I'll explain:

Cor... it's your heart!"

Gab became very serious again:

---

[2] A Latin word meaning 'heart'.

"The deepest recess of your heart. There... where the intimate and unique John is hiding! That's when the fighting begins:

Listen to Mike and you're listening to Life. Which doesn't just mean avoiding dying, from that dodgy shit, bought on the beach... "

He leapt to the next tree, to pick a wild strawberry. He sniffed it, moving his whiskers vigorously.

"Listening to Mike...

Is to be alive! Alive before! Long before... "

He hesitated to eat the strawberry.

"Here, this sweet treat is for you!"

Then he went on, weighing his every word.

"Beelzeb wants to seize your heart at all costs, so that you are his puppet!"

He became really serious:

"You are free Johnny! But it's a daily struggle, to resist this evil demon!"

"I think I have met someone who could understand." John murmured.

"Yes!" Gab cheered up between two new hazelnuts:

"You can found the "CordisClub"?"

He gave a perfect ballet jump, more than happy with his proposal!

God he was funny, bubbly, random...

Gab came back to sit down, a little out of breath:

"With her, and with your friends too, you will found the

CordisClub![3] I'm sure of it now!

You can leave the chocolate around the hazelnuts, I'll eat that too! Gab is greedy, Gab is a scholar, Gab loves Life and...

Gab loves his friends, John and Tatiana!"

Zoomy was barely surprised:

"Do you already know everything?"

Gab whispered mischievously:

"I see a lot of things from the top of my trees!"

He was silent for a long moment, then slipped between Zoomy's knees:

"It's time, I must leave soon. Even if I don't want to leave you! You know Johnny, I like playing the clown, I like laughing so much! But your fight will be a long one! You'll get yourself muddied a lot. Like me, when I've eaten too much and fall out a tree! Above all, never forget to go back to the bottom of your little cave, and ask Mike to...

Fart in Beelzeb's face!

Every time you ask him, he will!"

He smiled:

"With great joy even!"

He plunged back into an intense silence. One of those silences that's shared. That's a communion.

Then he looked at John, with an inquisitive eye:

"I have a secret to give you, before I leave. Not easy to listen to, the first secret of freedom!"

Then he came back to sit between John's knees, raising his

---

[3] Club of the Heart

jewel of a little head towards him.

"Are you… ready?"

"Yes, Gab, I trust you!"

"Here:

When something is kicking off, never look for fault in others, but only in yourself!"

He became cheerful again:

"Johnny, you'll see, you'll save a lot of time!"

With a sigh:

"Besides, no one can change other people, who are just as free as you!"

He started waltzing again:

"Gab delivered his secret, Gab delivered his secret… but… Johnny is free!"

He stopped twirling suddenly, for he noticed that John had become dark and tormented: "Look, this has nothing to do with guilt! I feel like you're swimming in that, deeply?"

"Jimmy… I… Jimmy… I should have, I could have…"

"Stop, stop, stop! This is one of Beelzeb's most subtle tactics:

He baits you, draws you in with his claws, pushes you into a whole heap of shit, and instead of congratulating you, he has a go at you! And there, did you see it, Johnny? Were you no longer in communion with me? You were engulfed in guilt and isolation! No, no, no, and no!"

Gab almost got angry, but soon he pulled himself together, and danced again:

"Gab dances and laughs and doesn't give a damn about

Beelzeb! But no! Gab is smart too!" He gave John a big wink:

"And... Gab never gives up!"

When he had finished his demonstration of spellbinding talent, he climbed squarely onto John's lap and placed his own little hand on his:

"Never condemn others! But neither should you ever condemn yourself! Otherwise Beelzeb's too happy!"

With his miniscule fingers he patted his friend's hand:

"Go down quickly into your deep little heart and call Mike to your rescue! Like calling up your best friend:

"Mike, I've done another stupid thing, help me!""

Gab was silent...

He did nothing but contemplate John, with his very sweet and persuasive eyes:

"Mike never gets tired of your return. He's waiting for you…"

He burst into loud laughter!

"And there... right there... K.O. Beelzeb! No chance!

Give me the rest of the chocolate bar. I'll eat it tonight, partying with my friends!"

"What are you celebrating?"

"Idiot, your entrance to the CordisClub!"

He intoned:

"Johnny is one of us! Johnny is one of us...

I have a nice voice, right?"

"You're the purest wonder I've ever met, Gab!"

Gab made a few light jumps in search of a violet:

"Here, take her this violet from me!"

He thought for a second:

"I'm talking too much! Actually... I give seminars every summer and... she was there!" Johnny smiled tenderly:

"In the Swiss Alps?"

"Yesssssss! You could go with her in July and admire..."

John interjected:

"How the peaks make love with the clouds?"

Gab nodded his graceful little head.

"Too bad, that you can't contemplate that from the top of a tree! That is heaven pal!"

Slowly he began to walk away.

"You're my friend John."

He returned once more, before going back to his tree:

"We are a chain, and each link is joined, invisibly to the other. John, you'll never be alone again!"

John had tears in his eyes:

He felt in the depths of his heart such a sweet unknown warmth.

Gab dawdled, stopped, sang a little, came back:

"John, never, never, never give up!"

Finally, he darted forward passionately and shouted:

"Forest, trees, leaves, ants, insects, fallow deer, hares, foxes, you, the handsome black one:

Welcome our friend John to CordisClub!"

Then he disappeared into the branches, like a star of fire, in the astonished sky...

...

5. CordisClub

When John returned home, he took his exercise book. His damned exercise book! The empty book, empty of words and empty of anything. And with a single stroke of his pen he recounted his meeting with Gab. Their conversation and...

The fight that, alongside Mike, he was going to spearhead against Beelzeb!

...

What happened... happened:

Zoomy, the essay-writing dunce, received his High School's first prize!

Tatiana was jubilant:

"Johnny... I'm inviting you to a "chip party" to celebrate that!"

"But your prevention?"

"My prevention is not imprisonment! Come on!"

John watched her enjoy one chip after another. Never had

he seen anyone enjoying chips, with so much delicacy, as if they were a fancy dish! So instead of gulping his down, as usual, he took his time. Those chips had a special flavour, a new flavour. He wished they could keep filling their stomachs forever. It was also his first bit of laughter, since Jimmy's death...

"I'm going to invite you to my house tomorrow for a very healthy meal!"

Tatiana laughed softly:

"And..."

She paused. For the first time, she was searching for words. John heard himself answer, as in a dream:

"Are we going to write the CordisClub charter together?"

Tatiana returned a starry smile.

"Johnny, yes... What happiness!"

"Are you… on the pill? Or do you have some condoms?"

Tatiana burst out laughing:

"Do you want to write the CordisClub charter with condoms? I think my computer will suffice!"

She looked at him lovingly:

"Listen John, I have nothing against sex! When we're ready, when we're sure..."

Her eye twinkled, a little like Gab's:

"We'll make love…"

...

The group of friends had been scattered since Jimmy's death.

There were also the police questions. Jimmy's father's

questions…

It was a very trying time for everyone. The kingpin's disappearance had left a strange void. It was he who had always indicated, what to do with each new threat...

John was aware of this and he called Paulo:

"Paolo, are we meeting at Ginkgo's tonight?"

…

"You better?"

"No, man... no! The pissing cops, the Blowjob Queen who blubs without stopping, it sucks mate! It really sucks!"

John took a deep breath:

"I…

I think I'm going to make some life changes!"

"Change what? You're scared because of Jimmy or... "

He forced out a laugh, but without conviction:

"Is it because of the bitch, who failed to revive Jimmy, when he arrived at the emergency room?"

"Paulo, she wasn't even there! And besides, this girl has a name, it's Tatiana!"

"Sorry, chief... I think I'm jealous. You're always with her, that's what it is!"

"Paolo, you remain my friend, more than ever…

Paolo, with Tatiana, we're forming a kind of club."

"Club?"

"Wait, let me finish:

A club where... you know... where...

Where we meet with our hearts?"

He paused, relieved that Paolo didn't laugh:

"You see, stop with all this playing once and for all. Stop running after…

After what is in the end nothing!"

He looked at his friend:

"Basically, we don't even know each other!"

Paolo didn't blink an eye. He was smoking one cigarette after another.

"You're my mate Paolo, but what do I know about you? Paolo, would…

Would you come to this club?"

"I don't know, man! Too much shit in my head!"

"So, do it for me:

Come to Ginkgo's on Saturday, have a drink with Tatiana!"

"It's on, see you Saturday!"

…

It was a Tatiana, superbly disguised as a geisha, who greeted John:

"What's this get up?"

John was stunned. It must be said that she was dazzling!

"I dive into my Japanese roots, whenever possible. We're nothing without roots! And anyway… it seems I had a geisha great-grandmother!"

John kept staring at her throughout the meal…

"Your sushi is so good!"

"I'm going to make you Japanese tea now, like Mum did."

He was surprised at himself:

"You do realise, I don't even want a fag?"

"When you give up smoking, we'll have a race. From the river to the cave!"

With a radiant pout:

"I swear you'll beat me!"

"Doped up with your great wine? Yep, it's a done deal...

I spoke to Paolo. He's not convinced, but he agreed to come to Gingko's on Saturday!"

"Me, I contacted Josiane and..."

"What! The Blowjob Queen, you speak to her?"

"Why wouldn't I talk to her? John, I'm not better than her, and we're all in the same boat!"

"Really, you still manage to amaze me, my goodness!"

She sighed:

"That wasn't my goal! Josiane... I repeat Josiane agreed to come to the first evening!"

She sat down in front of her cup of fragrant tea:

"I've been thinking about the charter, shall we set to work? At the first meeting, we'll have to explain what CC is! The abbreviation of CordisClub, and with your magnificent essay, it's really up to you, to do it!"

John felt flattered:

"I feel proud!"

"Yes but... it's not a game you know?"

"I know..."

She turned her computer on:

"I thought of having six or seven essential principles:

In fact, I already have six!"

"I'm listening to you little enchantress!"

She smiled and wrote aloud:

CordisClub Charter.

1.   No hypocrisy.
2.   Listen to Mike.
3.   Wage war against Beelzeb.
4.   Win your heart back.
5.   Give Nature back its kingship.
6.   Respect others.

"But something is missing, for the conclusion?"
John cried out as if he'd been waiting just for this.
"Seven: Never give up!"
Tatiana started dancing:
"With that we have our constitution, great!"
Johnny continued, sharing a tender thought with his friend:
"That's exactly what Gab is going to teach in his seminar in July!"
He put his hand on hers.
"By the way… I'll be accompanying you!"
He divined a tear of enchantment in the corner of her eye…
"We can treat ourselves to an apricot sorbet and a good glass of Yuzu!
And then… I have a fab movie if you want to watch it with me?"

This is how Tatiana spent the rest of the evening, huddled in John's arms, watching: *Memoirs of a Geisha*[4] ...

...

---

[4] A 2005 Rob Marshall film

6. Welcome to the Club

While crossing the park, to go to Gingko's, John took pleasure in taking his time. He paused, to listen to a robin. Often raising his head, hoping to see one of Gab's friends...

Paolo arrived late:

"I slept badly, but I did something amazing! Something my grandfather told me!"

"Welcome to the club!" John thought, "he never told me he had a grandfather!"

It's something, for if you can't sleep at night. Something to teach you patience!"

"Tell me! For once, I'm impatient!" replied Tatiana.

"You go out, you go to a field, or to a patch of garden. You get a stick, hit the ground and... you wait! But hey guys, you wait, without moving! And when any kind of insect, or worm, comes out, you make no noise. You follow it!

It moves forward, you go forward.

It recoils, you recoil.

It stops, you stop..."

He burst out laughing, pure Paolo laughter!

"At last!" rejoiced John, "I have that laugh again!"

"Last night, it was a caterpillar. I followed it for two hours with the torch on my iPhone! I swear that I slept fine, when I got back into bed!"

"Paolo!" exclaimed Tatiana:

"Are you inspired or what? That's exactly, what we want at the Club!"

She rose to kiss him:

"To share things, to know the other, their history, their culture!"

But a shadow that John knew only too well, froze on Paolo's face:

"You know, I'm black, and no one gives a toss what I say! I come from a race of slaves, colonised, despised. It's only when I shout, that I get listened to!"

John held his breath. Tatiana went red, which never happened to her.

"So, right there you're talking downright shit! Total shit!"

John jumped: Tatiana being rude?

"Listen mate, my great uncle was a kamikaze pilot. He crashed voluntarily onto a boat, filled with young people, like you and me! Does that make me a murderous fanatic?"

Paolo was about to answer.

"Wait, wait, I'm not done:

And what about John's Christian grandfather? Millions of

Christians have been - still are in some countries - martyred since Christ died on the cross? You'll never hear him talking or moaning about it.

And the Jews? Deported by the millions, exterminated?

Armenians, uprooted up until their graves?

And so many others?"

She was breathless:

"Women? The number of women tortured every day across the world..."

She drank a little water, caught her breath.

John saw that she had tears in her eyes.

"Paolo...

All of us have a reason to not move forward. To wade through our ancestors' pasts, which we don't care about anyway! Just like we'll always have a wound that needs healing, an excuse not to become alive! To enter into communion:

First with oneself, then with others. And of course, with nature as you did last night, with your friend the caterpillar!"

She put her hand on his: "Paolo, if we...

The future of this land that is mistreated yet so sublime...

If we continue to gorge ourselves with our moans, it's over! And that's CordisClub, precisely! The common fight, against the demon of discouragement and the demon of isolation! Helping each other beyond anything that enchains, destroys, blackens!"

She laughed:

"Or yellows...

Paolo, I'm not asking you to join us, but... "

She flashed her starry smile:

"That would be great! John loves you so much! And as for me, I want to take a stick and strike a piece of earth with you, to learn patience!"

When she had finished her fiery tirade, John realised that for the first time in his life, he was in love.

And ready.

Ready to make Love…

…

7. Mike

It had snowed a lot. The sky was ebony and the night frosty.

Inside the largest fir tree in the forest, Gab was working noiselessly in his cramped hollow. His darling was already asleep:

"She must rest, she is fragile!"

Gab lit up:

"Here she's much better off, I'm taking care of her!"

He rubbed his tiny hands together, with a slight smirk:

"It's also why, she chose me, rather than the beautiful black one, always obsessed with his charms!"

He pulled himself together:

"That's not all there is Gab, to work!"

From a pile of twigs, he pulled out a silver book and a green bottle:

"It's very successful, this green ink that I've simmered, and it feels so good!"

He sniffed the bottle. He wanted to dance:

"Gab is good! Gab made ink with essential oils! That do so much good to my little darling's lungs!"

He turned around and went to check that she was sleeping. With his nimble fingers, he pulled the woven dry moss blanket, right up under her neck. Then he went to fetch a fir tree branch and added it to the moss:

"It will be cold tonight my sweet, my own beautiful one."

He sat down to contemplate her and sang with a barely perceptible voice:

"My sweet, my little love..."

Then he straightened up:

"So...

This seminar on the passions?"

He smiled, like a little monkey:

"I will take these main characters:

The Queen-Mother: HRH Selfishness.

Then the princes and princesses... "

He smiled:

"They think they are unbeatable! That will be good to watch!

So, their nicknames:

Gluttony,

Greed,

Fornication,

Anger,

Sadness,

Despondency

And…

The Prince Consort: Pride!"

He threw his two adorable arms upwards in an amused sigh:

"What a programme!"

He got up, lifted up some big oak leaves and took some nuts:

"It makes me hungry!"

He dipped his index finger, as if it were a feather that had been sharpened, into the bottle that filled the whole hollow with perfume. He applied himself, to do some good writing: "The passions…

I need the red, the red bottle!"

He started again in red:

"The passions, if we repress them: it's sickness! If we suppress them: it's death!"

He nodded his graceful little head, rolling his eyes in all directions:

"Well said Gab! Keep going!

So, the passions, you have to…

Master their energies and transform them into creative energies…

There, Gab has the cor of his seminar!"

He closed his bottles and put the silver book back in its place.

It was necessary to be tidy in the winter cavern, because the space was just millimetres.

"I'll let all that hibernate."

He was conscientiously munching on his third nut, when lightning suddenly lit up his heart:

"And if I asked Georgy for a few short interventions? He's the specialist of the human soul, right? To keep it alive, I'll also recount my funny stories!"

He pushed his nose right into the bark of the big tree, so as not to make any noise with his jubilant laughter:

"And there, Beelzeb, nailed, done for! K.O.!"

He took to his feet with confidence.

"If it needs doing, then it will be done..."

He stuck his nose out of the entrance to their miniature cave. The sky was black ink. The stars were immense. They lit the frosted branches, like hundreds of arms, frozen in prayer.

Gab thought of Jimmy:

He sent him his tenderness and compassion...

Then he stuck his head out a little more, for a black shape had moved to the top of the neighbouring tree:

"No, but look at that, the handsome black one is performing his live open-air display! Whatever! And when he gets sick, I'll be the one who takes care of him again with my herbal teas."

He wriggled with pleasure! Sprinkled with stars, him too.

"I understand why Raphaela chose me...

MOI!"

Then, he closed up the hollow with the moss, which he had kneaded himself, with the fine sand. He decided to go to bed. He wrapped his little arm around Raphaela, gently pressing himself against her. And he let himself slide into the stars...

...

Up there, much higher than the beautiful black one, much higher than the fir trees, much higher than the stars ...

Mike was tilting his gold and diamond curls, with a smile of divine tenderness, for these two entwined little creatures. And he sent them a little of his breath, to warm them ...

...

PART TWO

MEETINGS

8. Gab's Seminar

Gab leaps to the desk. He stretched out his two graceful arms like a ballet dancer:

"Welcome everyone!

In this seminar, we will try to discern the energies that are harming you. Often without your knowledge. Or worse, those that launch you into reactions that are out of control. To you all, I spoke about the sublime gift of freedom. This allows you to spot the suggestions that besiege your heart. Some of them are evil, hence the importance of stopping them in their tracks.

These are very serious subjects! So much so, we should not take ourselves so seriously. A reason why we need to make way for transparency, sharing and humour!

Now, I'll leave it to my friends, to briefly introduce themselves, and the topics they want to cover.

In this order:

John, Tatiana, Paolo and Josiane."

"I'm John, a teenager who was lost, welded to his friends by orgies:

hard porn, alcohol, drugs, bingeing…

Hampered by my own complexes, I was fascinated by Jimmy's sexual prowess. Both of us, had been groomed by predators. We were making money, by keeping watch in front of the buildings, where drugs were being trafficked. I was constantly lying to my parents and using vulgar vocab, to wow my friends. After Jimmy's fatal overdose, I was crushed by pain. And remorse …

Especially since that evening, I wasn't hanging with him. I was visiting my grandfather at the home."

He paused for a few moments:

"In fact, I could have died in his place! Or with him …

I started then, to listen to the one who became my girlfriend, Tatiana. That is why I want to share with you, the experience of listening. Listening to others, but also to the signs that life offers us, from the bottom of the abyss…"

"It's me, John's Tatiana!

My mother, a Japanese woman, was run over by a drunk driver, when I was 15. Completely broken, I rushed into a world that was ugly and lugubrious. On the lookout for atrocities, both in the news and in culture. I even attempted suicide …

Then, I had the chance to work with a wonderful psychotherapist and I agreed to live again, by helping others:

I became a nurse …

I'd like to discuss with you, victory over depression,

46

seeking the gift of life in every detail…"

Paolo came to the desk, with his big, awkward body and his impish smile:

"I loved the same vices as John. I'm his best mate!"

He offered his first burst of laughter: "He's the one who got me into this trap, when last summer we were having a blast with orgies! As you can see, I am black and I struggle to find my place. Far from my roots, especially from my grandfather, the village sage. You know, we don't listen to old people here anymore! I would like to reveal to you some customs he passed on to me, when I was a child … "

"Don't be shocked, I'm the one they called:

The Blow Job Queen! As you can see, I'm no oil painting, so, my sexual offerings were my way of being recognised by the group. Especially by Jimmy who I was in love with. Anyway, I'm carrying his child … "

She paused between two sobs:

"Tatiana came to meet me and invited me to an evening at CordisClub. I was floundering so much that I accepted, not really believing in it. Since joining CordisClub, I finally have a family!

I would like, during this seminar, to understand, why I despised my body so much … "

"There you are, my dear participants, these are my friends!"

Gab gave one of his enchanting jumps:

"Not brilliant eh?

However, to be cured, we must first, as our friends have

done, recognise that we are sick. This disease is nested above all in the deep heart. Also, we must learn to protect it. In order to experience true fellowship with one another. I emphasize the word "experience": Anything that you can't experience, in this seminar, chuck it in the bin!

Meditate tonight on these first steps...

I would now like to introduce you to my Raphaela and our first

Son, little Uriel."

Raphaela, frail and full of grace, got up onto the desk. She snuggled against Gab.

On her back was fastened a mini squirrel, not at all frightened.

It was the first time, the friends had seen Raphaela, and their eyes filled with delight.

"She is my haven, my enchantment!" Gab rejoiced:

"She will listen to you with her tenderness and you will love her ..."

...

The meal took place in serene happiness:

Little Uriel jumped on all the knees there, asking for treats.

The CordisClub friends took care to involve the new participants and Raphaela, looking at Gab with a knowing eye, hummed happily. Then, the squirrel family went to bed in a big oak tree, while Tatiana went to the village pub to serve as a translator for a group of Japanese people.

John and Paolo decided to go for a walk by the mountain

lake, darkened by nightfall.

"Bravo CordisClub!

Josiane did not have an abortion and chose to raise Jimmy's son, alone.

Frankly mate, I'm not sure that's so great!

Mate…

Do you remember when you were having a right old laugh last year?"

Paolo lit a cigarette. He drew a big puff:

"Me, I have no one and now that all these feelings of pleasure have built up in me, my body is wanting to take over! Get it?"

He threw away his cigarette.

"I mean, that shit, I still need it!"

"I get you, mate. For me it's simpler:

Because I'm so happy with my Tatiana. I love her and I've learned to make love, not just to fuck! But… Paolo, don't give up! I beg you! Not now…"

On the lake could be seen the reflections of the stars, so many flames in sumptuous ball gowns. Waltzing to the sound of an imperceptible melody, coming straight from the sky.

"Shall we swim?"

They plunged into the icy, ebony water. Despite the cold, they swam side by side. A rhythmic and silent swim.

And it was a delicious moment of pure friendship…

When John went upstairs, Tatiana had not yet come home. He decided not to wait up for her and lay down, meditating on Gab's words, before falling asleep...

...

9. The Old Seated Giant

When he woke up, Tatiana was already dressed. She had put on her pink canvas hat, the one that made John smile, and tease her: "My old Japanese tourist!"

"Are you going out?"

She sat on the edge of the bed:

"A Japanese medical student, at the faculty Mum visited, would like to climb Devil's Peak."

John got up and took her in his arms:

"I am going to miss you!"

"I'll be home tonight, darling. In addition, you'll have a nice surprise today!"

She kissed him quietly, took her backpack and went out.

"Where's Tatiana?" Paolo asked.

"She's introducing a lost Japanese guy to the secrets of the Alps..."

Raphaela and Gab arrived in their turn, without little

Uriel who was still sleeping.

"My friends, for the theme of the harmful energise that enslave the heart, we are going to welcome one of our annual guests. His great age and experience will be precious to us."

He gave a cheeky hop:

"You see Paolo, we can listen to old people too! My friends, here is our faithful Senior: John Senior!"

John held his breath.

The door opened, and a giant in a wheelchair slid to the desk.

"Grandpa?" John exclaimed.

"Yes, my Johnny, it's me!"

An angel passed. One of sacred silence…

The giant old man, nailed down in his infirmity, radiated luminous serenity:

"My children, let me introduce myself:

In our family, of an Orthodox faith, our faith was limited to social custom. After my studies, I wanted to make a pilgrimage to the Holy Mountain[5]. A mountain that has been welcoming monks since the 9th century. I fell in love with it spiritually! So I decided to go home, to announce that I was going to become a monk. But then, on the return trip, I ran into my Helen and... I realised that my way would be through marriage!"

Paolo stood up:

"Grandpa...

---

[5] Mount Athos in Greece. Reserved only for Orthodox men.

Do you still love your Helen?"

"She fell asleep two years ago. I cherished her until her last breath..."

He stopped, his eyes brimming with memories:

"You know Paolo, it was about that too, keeping the gift of Love.

In the Orthodox marriage service, the bride and groom do a turn around the gospel three times:

A sacred dance that never stops. Thanks to it, I continue in hope."

"Grandpa, I have a remark you might not like. "

"At my age, nothing holds fear anymore Paolo, go ahead!"

"In my village, we kill each other in the name of God! And this is nothing new in the history of religion ... "

"Your remark Paolo brings me to the heart of our subject: Evil does not exist!"

"Maybe not for you, Grandpa?"

"I mean Paolo, that these deviations, that torture our souls and our bodies, have no essence. It is man, this free creature, who chooses to disconnect his energies from the source of Life. His soul then sets out in search of other energies, some of which are devastating. And the peak of this devastation is to take life! This religious tolerance didn't invent itself Paolo, it was won. Not forcibly through ascetic pursuits, but above all through the intimacy of a personal relationship, which can only be triggered by a loving encounter with God. Because, what lover would want to destroy anything, while his heart is filled?

My children, I beg you:

Whether you are believers or atheists, learn to love life! But this life that will get the best out of you. The one that will educate you to respect other cultures, beliefs other than your own. I promise you will always be a winner!"

"And, Grandpa, what do you think about absolute freedom of expression?"

The old man did not answer. He tilted his head, his eyes closed ...

"Paolo, freedom of expression has been achieved through huge sacrifices that date back in history..."

Again he tilted his head, silent ...

"It's a sacred conquest! But despite this we immolate it on the altar of blasphemy? By tearing hearts, under the pretext of making others laugh? Everyone must respond to them with their conscience.

Myself, I invite you to join the one holy war:

The one against all kinds of inner demons, which ravage the heart and can lead it to perform monstrosities:

Against others or...

Against itself!

And now my little ones, I must return to my care home..."

Josiane got up:

"Grandpa, how do you, helpless and widowed, stay so happy?"

The grandfather began to laugh:

"One of my English friends used to say:

"If you cannot avoid it, enjoy it!"

More seriously, let's just say that my time spent on the Holy Mountain has left its mark. Everyone has total freedom to choose their port. But I strongly encourage you to seek yours!"

No one wanted to get up. A few more moments, with the old giant, whose abundance of life far exceeded infirmity …

Then Gab jumped on Grandpa's shoulder:

"It is precisely this war on evil spirits, that we are going to talk about! Thank you grandfather, for this intense testimony!"

John could only confirm:

He thought not of freedom of expression, nor of fanaticism, nor of demons. He only had one obsession:

What was Tatiana doing at Devil's Peak with that dirty Jap!

Paolo got up again, embarrassed:

"I would like to say that I'm drooling! I have a body, to be more precise a sex, that claims its due. Masturbation with pornographic fantasies, I still have a need for it."

Gab looked at Paolo with his affectionate little eyes:

"What a sincere confession Paolo! There is nothing abnormal in what you are talking about. Just that you've been stuffed with pornography, orgies, that corrupt nature and make it uncontrollable. Well beyond natural desires."

"I can no longer go back to how things used to be?"

"No… And don't feel guilty, when these reflexes arise. Try to get rid of these memories of lust as much as possible.

Continue to let off steam in sport. And prepare a nest in your heart, for a companion whom you will cherish, and who will cherish you! "

He leapt up onto Paolo's shoulder: "Don't give up, your sincerity will bear fruit!"

"I'm hanging on Gab, I trust you!"

"Dinner!" Raphaela called:

"A meal, simmered by our Paolo, who has energies to spare!"

...

10. Malevolent Suggestions

In the evening, when Tatiana came home, John was waiting for her.

She didn't kiss him and didn't say a word.

"Something wrong, Tatiana?" "

She sighed:

"I don't know John, I…

It was wonderful to speak Japanese. The first time since Mum…"

"It's okay, babe, it's just that you…"

He paused, caught his breath:

"You're not falling in love with this student?"

"I don't think so, but I'm upset!"

"Shall we go for a walk?"

"No, I beg you, leave me alone, to sort my head out!"

John went out and instead of walking, he started running

around the lake, a sombre, diabolical abyss. He ran, so as not to think. He ran, so as not to scream. He did not even notice a couple in front of him, who were walking peacefully. He passed them and heard Paolo's laughter:

"Are you running a marathon mate?"

John stopped. It dawned on Paolo quickly:

"Are you not okay? In any case, if you're running at this hour of the night, something's screwed up, I know you!"

Josiane rested her hand on Paolo's shoulder:

"Leave him be Paulo, I think he needs to be alone!"

"Thank you, Josiane! You two, carry on! Tomorrow, everything will be fine!"

He finished his lap of the lake and came back to the bedroom. He felt disturbed. He needed to know, to question, but Tatiana had already fallen asleep…

…

On the third day, she did not get up for the session. She used the pretext that she knew the subject. John went to the seminar room alone again, and sat down at the far end. In front, he saw that Paolo was whispering in Josiane's ear.

"Today my friends, we will approach, in a simplified way, the theme of the bad passions:

The Queen-Mother of these passions is selfishness:

Not only a perverse and excessive love of oneself, but also an anguish in the face of suffering, in the face of death or quite simply in the face of the future. We then try to pacify it with more and more distractions We are not here on the register of deviant morality. We are the source of what went wrong:

The break with the source of Life.

This same queen-mother in turn perverts the princes and princesses:

Gluttony, greed, jealousy, anger, sadness, despondency, violence, pornography, fanaticism and many more.

Seconded by her husband, the consort:

The great prince of pride, who is not only dazzled by himself, but hates penance…"

Delighted and mischievous, he jumped on the desk:

"I'm going to tell you a little story:

We are in winter, in a hut belonging to a very poor peasant couple.

On their meal table they only have some miserable soup and a piece of bread. From the neighbouring hut comes a strong smell of sausages. Food that the poor peasant woman loves! They were crumbling their bread in silence, when all of a sudden a fairy appeared, saying to them:

"You are entitled to three wishes, in a row. No matter what your requests, they will be granted."

Immediately the peasant woman asked, that the sausages from the neighbouring hut be put on her plate. Furious, her husband exclaimed:

"Hang those sausages from my wife's nose!"

I'll leave you to imagine, what the third wish was!

Through this story, we can underline, that everything starts with a suggestion. Then the action follows…

So vigilance is needed, as soon as the suggestion shows

itself:

Anger, gluttony, jealousy...

Here, another story, on the theme of jealousy:

Two friends, well they called themselves friends, were constantly jealous of each other:

As soon as one had something, the other wanted it.

One day, a fairy came to meet them:

"You have the opportunity, to make one wish each. Choose anything you want, it will be answered. Provided that he who has made the wish knows that his friend will receive it twofold!"

The tormented pair did not open their mouths. Already enraged, with the thought of the other receiving double...

At last, filled to the brim with hatred, one of them exclaimed:

"I want to lose an eye!"

My friends... Hell is at the door of the heart. That is why the prince of darkness sends you so many suggestions and urges you to enact them. That way you become his toy, as well as the prey of all predators! On the lookout for money, power or destruction! Are you tired? Should we stop?"

"No Gab," Josiane replied, "keep going!"

"So I'm going to sum this all up:

1. Remain vigilant and immediately cut off any suggestion at the root, before it has time, to prompt you to act!

2. If you can't, call Mike, or a listening ear, and confess! Yes, free your heart! Experience this, and you'll see the

relief it brings."

"Is that enough?" Paolo asked.

"It's not too bad! But don't forget the last point:

The one the prince consort hates! Let me illustrate it, with another little story:

A monk, who like all monks had taken a vow of chastity[6], came down to the town every week to sell the products of the monastery. One day, he ran into a beautiful prostitute and… desired her.

On his way back to the monastery, he struggled to remove this image from his heart. At each bend, Beelzeb appeared to him and whispered:

"She's beautiful, huh?

Couldn't you at least go to her once?"

Returning to the monastery, he didn't tell anyone about it.

So the demon continued to torture him, so that he became obsessed by this woman. The next week he went to find her and slept with her. Ashamed, he headed back home. Again, at each bend, the demon appeared. But menacing this time and questioned him, to make him feel guilty.

But the monk, experienced enough, understood his game…

"Hey... where are you coming from? "

"From the city, as I do every week."

---

[6] One of the three vows that monks take on entering their calling: poverty, chastity, and obedience.

"What did you do in the city? "

"I sold the products of the monastery, like I do every week."

"Aha ... and... what else?"

Beelzeb sneered with his blood-red fangs:

"What else?"

"Nothing."

"Nothing else? And this woman?"

The monk stopped:

"Which woman?

There isn't a woman!"

The demon went on at every turn. He was fuming, screaming, terrifying...

But the monk confessed nothing to him. At last on reaching the monastery, he ran to the Gerondas[7]. He confessed his sin to him, expressed his regrets, and became a very good monk again... Here my friends, this last point is essential:

Never allow Beelzeb to accuse you! But don't allow him to lock your heart into self-justification, either! That is, in his infernal kingdom of pride! Get rid of every mistake, whatever it is, with sincerity! No one is free from mistakes, no one is perfect! But sincerity is one of the avenues for liberation ...

Enough for today, we'll stop there ... "

---

[7] A hieromonk chosen by the monks to be their superior.

...

John left very quickly, avoiding the friends.

He went up to his room, recognising in his soul the sadness, anguish and anger ...

Tatiana was preparing her notes. She smiled at him. But her smile was tense and painful.

John tried to respect her melancholy and her silence…

At dinner, Gab realised that the couple was no longer the one he had known, so he placed himself between them. He, usually jovial and talkative, remained discreet, praying to the angel of love to protect them.

Raphaela looked at all three of them and she could not help but sing her tenderness.

Paolo and Josiane kept on feeding little Uriel and seemed to be floating in a light world...

...

11. Tatiana

She jumped, coquettishly, her adorable little snout in the air. She swung her orangey-red tail, slim and agile. She was ... irresistible:

Raphaela…

Proud to lead her little troop, on the banks of this mountain pool, which she knew by heart.

The green water, sometimes dark, sometimes slightly silvery, endeavoured to offer a warm welcome.

"This is the life we came here for!" Raphaela declared, inviting her friends to sit down:

"This pool will keep our secrets, and it will accompany us daily. To work my darlings! Who wants to start?"

"I love nature," confirmed Tatiana, "it calmed me down a lot when Mum had that fatal accident. My psychotherapist encouraged me to pursue this intimacy with the river, the forest, the animals. I ran into Gab there and life was able to take on a path that I never imagined…

With Gab, I learned to transform my own pain, soothing the pain of others. But also, I agreed to wake up to every little detail of the beauty of life:

A passing butterfly, the moment of a ray of sunshine. Birdsong. My dog's amusing expression as he waits for his treat. That film that prompted a flow of tears of communion. The scent of grass on summer evenings…

So tonight, I invite each of us to meditate, on these thousand details that embellish our lives. Chasing away negative energies, always on the lookout."

"Me," interrupted John, "I draw! Like grandpa.

When he is too sad, because he misses his wife, they take him out to the garden and he draws. Always trying to draw something beautiful!"

"So we're pushing back?" Josiane said.

"It's not hiding the pain," commented Raphaela, "but about walloping it with a new chance at life!

That's the main thread of these workshops.

Turn a pain, a failure, into new luck.

However, one must also accept, that in order to get rid of the filth in the soul, it has to be drawn or described. Even with illustrations that are horrifying, but without trapping yourself in them while you consider them. Moreover, to grow, at some point, it will also be necessary to face the shadows of the soul. This will prevent them from reappearing without announcing themselves …»

"I would like to insist again," said Tatiana, "on the life-giving energy of work:

Work, whatever it is, structures the rhythms of life, binds people together, creates relationships and uplifts us!

Finally, I would like to talk about my difficulty in integrating the mystery of destinies, which suddenly take a direction so opposite to what we had planned. Because I am someone who likes to plan, manage and above all understand. With me, everything revolves around understanding. To reassure myself no doubt, that with a stubborn will, I will get to the bottom of it all!"

She sat down again, fragile but upright:

"Of it all…"

Raphaela applauded:

"Thank you Tatiana for this generous testimony!

That of not remaining paralysed in our sorrow, but of kind of "offering it", in the service of those who are experiencing trials. This makes it possible to realise immediately, that nobody has a monopoly on suffering, and this can get them out of an overwhelming sense of isolation. And then, what a sublime message, that of awakening to Beauty, to expel that which degrades, suffocates, or sullies! We will follow your invitation, and end the session with this meditation on the Beautiful." She smiled:

"My friends, I'd like you to offer yourself to Beauty's therapy:

In nature, in art, in every detail of our daily lives!

But also in the clothes you choose to wear, modelling yourselves on the bright colours of the flowers and birds!"

Raphaela paused. She toyed with some of her favourite

eyelash beats:

"The question remains:

Do we have to understand everything? Explain everything?

We'll try to see in our meetings, if there is not ever some mystery about it all that needs respecting. But for now, let yourself be carried away by the magnificence of this countryside…"

This stopover in the kingdom of the pool was prolonged, without anyone complaining.

Until the sky bowed down before the first star…

…

"Before going back, I would like to tell you a little story that Gab adores."

When pronouncing Gab's name, Raphaela sparkled, snatching supremacy from the beautiful star:

"In the depths of Alaska there were three hermit monks who lived in self-sufficiency. Immersed in nature and natural living. It was even said that they worked miracles, that they caught delicious fish that couldn't be found anywhere else.

One day a bishop, as incredulous of these legends as he was curious, decided to visit them. He was surprised to see that the three hermits, who were very hospitable, did not know the Scriptures or even the Lord's Prayer.

So he worked hard to teach them, which wasn't an easy task…

When the three hermits finally managed to recite the entire prayer, the bishop got back on his boat.

After about fifteen minutes at sea, he heard the hermits' voices calling out after him:

"Monseigneur, Monseigneur!"

He went up on deck and…

Was amazed to see the three hermits running on the water! When they got near the boat, they shouted out of breath:

"Monseigneur, Monseigneur, we have forgotten the end of the prayer!"

The dumbfounded bishop replied:

"Well it doesn't matter. Continue as you have been doing up until now!"

And he blessed them with a hand that was still trembling…

Up there, right up there, the star was laughing softly…

…

12. John

The next day, it was John's turn. He was not in good shape when he began his story:

"I never had any special concerns as a child. My mother was always there. Dad worked non-stop, but whenever he could, he paid us attention. In fact, my only great disappointment, was the arrival of my little brother.

He stole the show away from me. I was simply jealous.

As a teenager, I thought I was ugly. I had no success with girls, so I dealt with my sexuality on my own. This subject is too often crowded out:

Within the family or at school, with lessons solely focused on avoiding catching AIDS.

When all's said and done, us guys were created with dicks! This "taboo" goes away, when you're with friends! But not only that!

Look at how our senses, more precisely, our sex is constantly being teased by advertisements, magazines, films! So even during sport or meditation, it pursues us!

Sport…

I stopped playing it when I met Jimmy…

Jimmy:

A guy, a proper geezer! Beautiful as a god to boot! He rounded up all the girls and … I just had to try to follow. And that's where my life took a turn for the worse.

Extreme pornography.

Orgies.

Drinking.

And slowly… drugs. A hell that my parents, to whom I was constantly lying, didn't notice…

After Jimmy's death by overdose, I thought I was going to go too.

Luckily, I had met Tatiana shortly before. Despite everyone's mockery, I kept on seeing her.

I even started to listen to her, without admitting it. Without admitting it to myself…

She's the one who got me to Gab."

Raphaela couldn't help but start a little with pleasure:

"Our Gab!"

"This meeting was the turning point in my life. I just decided to trust Gab! To follow his advice, to get out of hell."

He sat back down. He looked soothed:

"To get out of hell."

"Wonderful!" cried Raphaela.

"You see my friends, an excruciating drama…"

She raised her eyes to the sky:

"Let the angels take care of Jimmy now! An excruciating

drama, which has been flipped like a pancake! But for that, John's participation was needed, who continued to see Tatiana, despite the taunts. And then, without trying too hard or explaining…"

She insisted:

"Nor understanding …

He obeyed Gab! This form of obedience isn't blind, but it springs from an intuition that right there, something is taking place that is over-taking the mundane!

It's good, John, that you broached the subject of sexuality. You are right, God did not create you angels, or disembodied beings. Our world is no more perverted than it was before, think about the Roman orgies! But it has the means to broadcast to everyone, even at the very moment of curiosity or need. Yesterday Gab evoked this 'detox' of speaking about it. To stem these parasitic thoughts, by confessing them. That includes this degrading pornography, as well as any form of violence."

Raphaela put on her most seductive smile:

"Because love, sharing and communion of bodies is not that…"

Paolo stood up:

"Well friends, help me find this communion! Withdrawal from drugs and alcohol is already a hassle, so for sex, I will have to be castrated!"

"Patience, handsome kid! Patience! Besides, tomorrow, if I'm not mistaken, you're going to teach us patience, right?

In the meantime, at John's request I will read you a poem:

71

A Smile, by Paul Eluard[8].

> *The night is never complete*
> *There is always, since I say it*
> *Since I affirm it*
> *At the end of sorrow*
> *An open window*
> *A lighted window*
> *There is always a dream*
> *Desire to fulfil, hunger to satisfy*
> *A generous heart*
> *An outstretched hand, an open hand*
> *Attentive eyes*
> *A life, the life to share."*

The little troop lingered dreamily until sunset…

"Let's go and find Gab, he went to teach little Uriel how to swim!" said Raphaela, with a touch of pride.

"Tomorrow, we'll find out how to become patient, with our Paolo…"

…

---

[8] French poet, 1895-1952

13. Paulo

Tatiana will not participate today, she is climbing Devil's Peak, with a befuddled Japanese guy!" John announced moodily.

"We will have to ask her, whether the Japanese guy was impatient about reaching the summit!" continued Raphaela, but only to bring back the good mood:

"So Paolo, over to you!"

Paolo got up. Slender and strong. In his hand, he held a long stick:

"This tactic was passed on to me by my grandfather, who was the village sage.

I would like to take this opportunity to say, how much I miss it, this passing on of traditions by the elders. What an amputation, to believe that we know everything, just by playing around on our computers!

So here is a way to learn patience, centred on nature:

I'm going to hit the ground and dig around, to find a fairly large insect. Then, I will follow him. I will try to move forwards, backwards or stay still with him.

Here's an ant colony! But they're too numerous and tiny…

Oh great, come see, the dream victim:

A huge beetle! A dung beetle in fact. Look, he's still shaping his dung and earth ball with the jagged edges of his head! Now I'm not moving a muscle…"

"Do you know what he'll do with it?" whispered Josiane.

"Yes, he's going to hide it, quietly eat it, and when he has fertilised impregnated his sweetheart, she can lay her eggs there too. We don't make any noise, we wait…"

The beetle continued its mobile construction. One strand after another. He carved in some height, adjusted the base and rolled it a little, to catch mud…

"Here we go! He'll push it backwards, with his long hind legs."

How long did it last? For the beetle too long probably, but for the friends, what a lesson!

"You've seen, how he gets knocked back, falls, gets up, starts again! Worse off than Sisyphus[9], this guy!"

"Paolo, you are fantastic!" said Raphaela, jumping on his shoulder:

"What an example of patience and tenacity! You see that nature is intelligent! As if an angel is stationed behind each

---

[9] A character from Greek mythology, condemned by Hades to spend infinity rolling a stone up a mountain and then falling back down as he reached the summit.

of its creatures!"

Despite the twilight, it was still very hot and Paolo was sweating.

"The green frog right there at the water's edge!" shouted Josiane:

"Paolo, what about following him too?"

Paolo didn't need asking twice:

He was approaching the pool when the frog began to croak vigorously. Paolo imitated him, but badly and he scared him. The frog leaped into the pool and disappeared into the reeds. Of course, Paolo also took off into the water, to general applause. When he came out, he sat on the floor, with his irresistible laugh. Josiane took his towel and began to dry him. Surprised, Paolo rested his head on Josiane's big belly. A loving spark...

Then he straightened up shouting,

"Hey ... it moved, the baby moved? I swear to you it moved!"

"This is the life that we have come here for," sang Raphaela, with emotion:

"Life..."

...

14. Kaori

On the road to the hostel, Tatiana wondered, why she had agreed to drive Kaori to Devil's Peak: "Especially since today I'd promised Paolo, to experience patience with him! Well, patience, I exercise it in my work!

But…

Raphaela? Josiane? John… it was me who steered them here, and I'm abandoning them?

No… I'm just putting myself in the service of a compatriot, who needs me!"

She felt that her analysis was a little off, but she didn't have time to rethink it:

He was waiting…

Equipped like a real mountaineer, wearing an appropriate backpack and alpine climbing shoes. With such an athletic body, on which was placed, as if in deliberate contrast, that…

She was looking for the word... angel's face? No, archangel's!

"Thanks for guiding me!" he said in Japanese.

Before starting the ascent, he listed all the surrounding peaks.

"You're well informed!" smiled Tatiana.

"I'm curious about everything! I also know the flowers and medicinal plants, that we'll come across."

Indeed, the climb turned into an encyclopaedic excursion! Tatiana was enjoying herself. She took it all in. She analysed her fascination:

"Me too, how I love to know everything! It's awesome!"

And without realising it, she in turn began to speak. But not of flowers, trees, or peaks.

She spoke in one fell swoop of her childhood, her mother's death, her holidays here, each year with her father, who this time had gone to Italy with his latest conquest ...

She told of everything, except for ... Gab of course!

She didn't talk about John either…

Kaori looked upset. He stopped, closed his eyes, and offered his face to the sun…

By God he was beautiful! Tatiana would never have known that one day there would be something as beautiful as the sun…

They resumed climbing. He told her about Tokyo, university, his family, Japan:

"Have you never been to Japan?"

"Not yet! But ... it's planned!"

She failed to specify, that it was planned with John! This "oversight" made her stumble on a big stone. Kaori picked her up and kept her hand in his.

"Understand immediately and react!" she screamed deep in her heart.

Eternity clung to them…

She felt not only her hand escaping from her, but something that was unbelievably capsizing too!

She withdrew her hand:

"We haven't arrived yet!"

She pulled her hat down over her eyes and thought:

"All the better, I can prepare my attitude!"

The sun was hitting them like a thousand thunderbolts ...

"We're going to drink a little!"

Kaori pulled out his water bottle:

"I have a surprise for you!"

He uncorked it and made her smell it:

"Yuzu, you're crazy! We'll be drunk, we have to go down again!"

Kaori laughed, with his teeth purer than all the neighbouring peaks.

"You don't say, I put a teaspoon in a litre!"

He looked at her, almost sadly:

"Besides, I'm already drunk:

Drunk on you…"

Then he added, as if it went without saying:

"Come to Tokyo, with me, tomorrow!"

Tatiana swallowed half the bottle in one go, then hurriedly started walking again:

"No, she hadn't heard!

No, she was going to move in with John at the start of the school year!

No, she didn't come here for…

For what?

For?

For…"

She couldn't find a word, or an explanation! She only found her heart, which was accelerating faster than her feet…

Upon reaching the summit, she was out of breath. Kaori moved behind her. She felt his long black hair, sliding over her neck. Then she understood …

That there was nothing to understand:

It was, what it was …

He took her face in his two slender, strong, and beautiful hands. He lifted her hat. It was she, who advanced her lips, to let herself be kissed…

Her plans, her analyses, vanished the very instant that, she was in his arms! Burned by that insolent sun! But Tatiana was sincere. She whispered in a cursed groan:

"Kaori, I didn't come here alone!"

They took their picnic in silence. Facing the Alps, a little embarrassed and dazed. The Alps that made love with the clouds…

When they came back down, their steps, their gestures were in perfect harmony. As if they'd been walking down together for centuries…

When they got to the hostel, he smiled at her:

"Thank you!"

Not a word more: it was, what it was…

He climbed the small staircase of the chalet. Very slowly…

Then he turned back round, his archangel's face almost awkward looking:

"Tomorrow I'll be here at 8.00 am, waiting for you…"

She remained in her upside-down state for a few more seconds…

Then she started to run. Gallop rather! To the edge of the pool.

Twilight had fallen. It was cool now. She threw her bag on the shore and plunged fully dressed into the water. She crossed the pool like a madwoman, frightening the last ducks, who were savouring the evening sweetness. When she came out of the water, she was shivering. She curled up, like a wounded animal and let out her sobs:

Unthinkable.

Inexplicable.

Unexplained…

But it was the first time in her life, that her sobs were good. Were hot, were soft, were …

Crazy…

…

When she got to the room, she was relieved because John was sleeping.

She slipped frozen, under her duvet. Eyes wide open.

For a long time, she tried to take back everything that had happened, trying to reason again and again...

Finally exhausted and defeated, she closed her eyes, and murmured in Japanese:

"Tomorrow I'm leaving for Tokyo!"

...

15. The Hurricane

When John got up, Tatiana had packed her suitcase.

"Tatiana? Tatiana?"

"Oh John, I… I am so sorry! I fought. I can't anymore…"

She was crying tears of despair. Tears of relief too:

"I would never have believed! Never… "

She stopped, breathed in deeply, then spat out in a single jet:

"I'm leaving for Tokyo!"

John was paralysed, like a concrete statue…

It was Tatiana, who had the courage to continue:

"Our story has been wonderful, but I can't resist anymore. It's not just him…

Everything is pulling me there… like an inevitable destiny."

The statue remained petrified.

"John, it's better you don't say anything! Continue your

journey with Gab and the club! I beg you… "

She took her suitcase, but did not put on her pink hat, for a storm was threatening.

"You are ...

You will always be John, and there will always be a place for you in my heart!"

She turned around and walked out.

The statue felt each part of him disintegrate, like a dismantled marionette:

Tatiana had closed the door.

Tatiana was leaving for Tokyo.

Tatiana had just left him…

He did not go downstairs to eat. He rushed straight to the village shop and bought two bottles of vodka. His old demons appeared and gave him signs of encouragement.

When he reached the lake, he collapsed on a bench ...

…

"Where are Tatiana and John?" Gab asked worriedly.

"I think I just saw Tatiana with her suitcase?" replied an astonished Raphaela.

Paolo jumped from his chair. He rushed up the stairs into John's room, climbing the steps four at a time. He shouted through the window:

"He's not in his room, but I know where to find him!"

When he arrived at the bench, John was embarking on his vodka therapy.

"What are you doing, John?"

"She is heading to Tokyo with her Japanese guy!"

"For God's sake, I'll smash that Jap bastard's face in!""

And Paulo's old demons, rejoiced in their turn, stoking the fire in his heart! What a contrast to Gab's harmonious agility, which flitted from one tree to another, to join the friends! He launched himself onto John's knees, from the last branch of a larch tree.

"Paolo, you have better things to do, than demolish the Japanese guy! Leave me with our friend…"

Gab didn't show reproach, or any signs of annoyance, he only snuggled against John, who dropped one of his Vodka bottles. The angel of silence slipped in, discreet. Gab begged him to drop the second bottle, and whispered the appropriate words to him…

"It's a big test John, as you step into the depth of your soul!

Into your soul's eye…"

With his tiny hand, he stroked his friend's cheek.

"John, she needs it… needs to find her past again, her roots!"

He fell silent, watching the second bottle fall…

The lake was blacker than black. A reflection of a sky that could not control its anger either.

"John, do something for me:

Take the Devil's Peak trail!"

"Redo the path upon which she fell in love? Are you kidding Gab?"

"No, I'm not kidding about it! Not at all!"

He looked at him with eyes of compassion:

"Walking with nature, it'll calm you down!"

John stood up.

He obeyed.

He did not want to do Devil's Peak at all, but he realised that now was the time, more than ever, to take Gab's advice: overcome his despair. His anger. So, he chose to obey. To obey the one he loved, and who knew.

Gab relieved, whispered:

"See you soon, I promised Uriel, I'd teach him how to climb trees by himself…"

…

16. Devil's Peak

John began the climb.

As the sky was very stormy, nobody was there.

"All the better," he thought, "at least I won't be meeting any Japs!"

At times, his head burst, at other times it seemed to have exploded already.

Emptied of everything.

Emptied of love.

Emptied of life...

He climbed at an impressive speed. The higher he climbed, the darker his heart and sky became.

"How could she? I...

I hate her! Yes, I hate her! With her saintly speeches! Dirty bitch! I hate her!"

He screamed, like a hardened fugitive.

The demon of anger was feasting. The demon of hatred urged him to root out the remnants of loving feelings from his heart. And impatiently the demon of despair waited for him, a few rocks away.

But…

Halfway there, he found himself face to face with a gigantic crucifix. He froze as if magnetised:

Christ had his arms outstretched.

Torn.

Tortured.

A flash of lightning slashed the night sky, and illuminated the face of the tortured one.

The rain, then the mixed-in hail, and a violent wind arose. Hailstones lashed John's face like dozens of sharp darts. Then John fell on his knees and grabbed both feet of the crucified one:

"But shit, You, You are the Son of God!

Me, I only have her!

Just her!

Understand? Do You understand that?"

The thunder echoed like a vulgar shout of diabolical laughter. The mountain vibrated and John was soaked.

The Son of God remained impassive…

Water ran down his face, over the drops of blood and the crown of thorns…

A gust knocked John over, and a new flash struck the sky. A flash of inner light then pierced John's heart:

"Gab?"

At once he rose like a madman, and began to leap from one rock to another. Sometimes stumbling in the mud, sometimes guided by the fire in the sky. He hurtled down the mountain, like a wounded animal, in a desperate flight. Forgetting his fury and his hatred, to shout only one word through the sharp hailstones:

"Gab, Gab, Gab?"

Arriving at the village, he continued his escape to the big oak, at the front of the hostel. The giant tree was unflinching, but neither Gab, nor Raphaela, nor little Uriel were there. He rushed to the stairs and passed Paolo, who was carrying a big towel and a blanket.

"Gab?" John asked breathlessly.

"Gab's okay, but Raphaela has fallen and... We don't know.

I'm just taking a blanket. They're in the seminar room. Josiane is taking care of Uriel and trying to get him to sleep..."

...

17. Anguish

Soaked through, rammed into the depths of anguish, John opened the door:

Raphaela was lying there.

Motionless.

It could hardly, but hardly be guessed that she was still breathing. At her side, stretched out as close as possible, was Gab...

Gab, like John had never seen him:

His eyes were stopped. Stopped by what remained of Raphaela's breath.

And in that eye, that cheerful and mischievous eye, John saw flow a big, a very big, tear...

Gab was crying.

To John the spectacle was unbearable.

He kept himself from screaming.

He kept himself from breathing.

He even kept himself from crying.

Devil's Peak, the mountain, the hurricane, Tatiana's suitcase, her defeated face, the Japanese guy, everything had disappeared. Disappeared with the wind, that fucking wind, that had tossed Raphaela to the ground!

Only the most frightful suffering remained:

that of seeing a loved one suffer!

For the first time in his life, John began to pray to the Christ:

"Myself, I don't care, I don't ask You for anything! Me, I accept that it's all nothing. Ridiculous! Grotesque! But save Raphaela! I beg of You, Save Raphaela!"

He paused, his eyes devoured by tears:

"If You save her, I promise to go to the Holy Mountain, after the seminar!"

Then, he took a chair and sat without making any noise, facing these two little creatures so fragile and so moving. Not knowing how to help, he renewed his prayer:

"Save Raphaela!"

At the end of his strength, he finished by falling asleep...

...

18. The Awakening

A huge noise woke him with a start!

Raphaela?

What a sublime awakening!

Raphaela, her little head on Gab's chest, was nibbling on a piece of hazelnut…

John knew one of the most intense joys of his life. Everything was bathed in sweetness, peace, light …

Even the sun was back, and its rays were warming the room affectionately.

Gab …

Once again, John had never seen Gab that way:

Gab was even more beautiful, more loving than ever. His eyes had been transfigured into two suns of love.

The din then?

It was Paolo who was building a little wooden house under the roof, to shelter the squirrel family.

Josiane came in with little Uriel, who ran to snuggle up to

his parents.

It was…

A pure moment of communion.

Of true love.

Of the truth of Love.

"My dear friends," announced Gab, beaming. "I propose that tonight we meet in the courtyard for a big party:

Raphaela and I will sing."

John went up to his room and collapsed fully clothed, on his bed.

He slept until evening …

…

After the meal, no one missed the summons:

Gab, a red cap on his head, pink sunglasses and a microphone in his little fingers, somersaulted with some attitude. He threw a second microphone to Raphaela who needed to hold it with both her hands. She was dressed in lace mini shorts and of course the T-shirt depicting Gab on stage[10]. They started by singing the CC[11] hit, the lyrics for which had been written by Josiane, with the music by John:

I tell you never give up!
We can show them guys,
Evil we despise.

---

[10] This T-shirt, along with all the other CC designs, is available to buy from www.mariaandreas.eu

[11] CordisClub

Whiskered or not,
Every soul gets a shot:
I tell you never give up!

Red, grey or black fur,
There is no one God prefers,
Please no more war,
Just light. And even more,
I tell you never give up!

Atheist, Muslim, Christian, Jewish,
Deep inside the same wish,
Let's try to forgive,
And really be creative!
I tell you never give up!

Choose to be respectful,
And remain peaceful,
Let's become brothers,
We'll sing together,
I tell you never give up!

Let's join the Club,
To kill Beelzebub[12]
The only enemy,
The only blasphemy,
I tell you never give up!

Come join our hearts,
To this beautiful earth.

---

[12] Or Satan, or Lucifer

We can show them, friend,
That it's not the end,
Because we will never, never give up![13]

A breathtaking repertoire followed!

God they were incredible:

Even the fragile Raphaela, strutted with an exuberant vitality.

Unexpectedly beautiful, with energy rediscovered one hundredfold.

"The new rap stars of CordisClub!" proclaimed Josiane:

"Applause!"

Then Paolo amused everyone, with his many African dance tricks.

John stayed with his friends. He felt much better. He realised then, that life was winning a new battle ...

...

---

[13] Composed in English by the author

19. Josiane

Along the path that lead to the pool, nobody spoke, after the emotions of the evening before.

Raphaela was not leading, but was huddled on John's shoulder. She cajoled him affectionately.

"I'm going to get started!" announced Josiane, once the little troop had installed themselves.

"Of course!" rejoiced Raphaela, "we are all ears!"

Josiane didn't know where to start. She'd put her two hands on her big belly and ... was waiting:

"I never knew my father. He dumped my mother as soon as he knew she was pregnant. My mother started drinking and got remarried to a bully.

When I was 16, my stepfather raped me!"

Everyone jumped.

"It went on for several months. I felt damaged, alone in the world. My mother was drinking and seemed to notice nothing. I was petrified and didn't have the courage to speak to anyone! One evening, in a bar I'd run away to, I ran into Jimmy. Love at first sight, while for him, I was nothing more than a girl added to his collection. However, he helped me a lot. Welcoming me into his studio, and even driving me to a social worker…"

She hesitated, then whispered:

"I never saw my stepfather, or my mother, again. In fact, I no longer have a family!"

"You mean you didn't have, because now, we're here!" Paolo corrected.

Josiane's face sketched out a smile:

"It was then that …"

She searched for her words:

"My own wrong decisions intervened:

Instead of agreeing to do a paid apprenticeship, offered by the social worker, I preferred working for a friend of Jimmy's. My job consisted of, finding candidates for our orgies, and organising drug deliveries."

She burst into sobs:

"There you go my friends, I …

Well there's no glory to it:

I had a good life, I went on holiday to the sea. I also became the nice fat whore of the group. Anyway, I'd felt dirty from the start, so, it wasn't such a huge change!"

John jumped up and took her in his arms:

"Josiane, Josiane, I'm ashamed too! Ashamed, for having asked you to pleasure me, during those disgusting orgies! Can you forgive me?"

"Can you forgive us?" Paolo, who stood up in his turn, raised the stakes.

Raphaela had the intuition not to intervene, and to let this little intertwined world, settle its scores…

Josiane pulled herself together:

"I told you, I take my share of responsibility. But, I'll continue the story of my fall:

During our last holiday in Spain, I stopped taking the pill:

I wanted a child by Jimmy. My own kid, so I didn't feel alone anymore.

You know the rest. I hope that my child will be able to forgive me one day. You cannot imagine, how it eats at me! I can cry whole nights through:

Another kid, who will only be raised by its slut of a mother!"

"Stop!" cried Paolo, "we're all slags! And… this kid, you won't be raising it all alone!"

However, Josiane had started shedding torrential tears, as if…

To free herself from a past that was too heavy!

Paolo got up and hugged her:

"I will always protect you, from now on!"

Raphaela decided it was her turn to intervene. She leapt onto a small mound, facing the friends. She swung her two fragile and pretty arms:

"Josiane, I begin with my admiration. What a "cleansing!"

You knew how to vomit your ordeal up to us, without forgetting your share of responsibility for it, which is so rare!

You went from the state of a crushed victim, to that of an active actor. I'd even say "activated." Activated by this ability to see yourself as you are. Without any cheating, or embellishment!

And so my friends, permit me to go back to my main theme:

Once again it's an unbearable ordeal, out of which light gushes!"

She jumped in a cuddly manner and hugged Josiane's shoulder:

"You are here now, with your new family and ..."

She laughed heartily:

"Paolo as a bodyguard!"

Despite her acquiescence, Josiane continued to moan, like a frightened child...

Suddenly, she exclaimed, pointing her finger towards the forest:

"There was a dwarf over there, I saw a dwarf!"

Raphaela bounded across like an arrow.

"Calm down!" whispered Paolo, "calm down!"

"No, no, I'm telling you that I saw a dwarf!"

Raphaela approached, all wriggles:

"A real dwarf, are you sure, Josiane? Can you describe it?"

"Yes, he had a big red cap, a beard down to his shoes. And in his hand he was carrying a bouquet of plants."

Raphaela was amazed. She waggled her whiskers all over the place. She was waving her tail. Blinking with her long eyelashes. She climbed back onto the mound:

"It's Spiridonos! My friends, this has never happened before! Josiane's heart knew with so much integrity, spurting out her pain and her own mistakes, so that her eyes were..."

Raphaela paused for a long time. One of those "à la Gab pauses."

"Her eyes were purified, and she could see, what no one sees. Yes, Josiane saw a dwarf!" "Seriously?" asked Paolo:

"Are we all having a laugh here, what on earth?"

Raphaela leapt onto the big oak tree, at the edge of the forest and cried out, as loud as she could:

"Spiridonos, Spiridonos! It's me, your Raphaela!"

With that the ferns parted and what appeared but ...

The dwarf!

Raphaela descended at full speed. She ran to throw herself into the arms of this creature, smiling and cheerful.

"Raphaela, my darling how are you?"

The friends were transfixed. They were barely breathing.

"We are all fine, Spiridonos! And go figure this, one of our friends has received the grace, to see you! My darlings, I present the dwarf Spiridonos to you!"

The dwarf raised his long beard a little, and bowed:

"Raphaela's darlings are mine too!"

Raphaela did not want to lose this incredible chance. She hastened to add:

"As our Josiane was able to see you, I'm asking you to do the favour of welcoming the whole group, tomorrow at the cave!"

Raphaela multiplied her sets of eyelashes. She even started

dancing, lifting Spiridonos' beard.

"She is still just as bewitching!"

He was laughing:

"But so real, so cute, so kind!"

He stooped down, to take her in his arms:

"Of course, and since the request comes from you, I don't even have to wait for Abba Barnabas's consent. You will come to the cave tomorrow at the same time, go round the back! I will wait for you."

Big kisses, caresses, jubilation…

"See you tomorrow, my Spiridonos, see you tomorrow!"

She stood up straight, resplendent:

"It's Gab, who's going to be blown away!"

Spiridonos then lit up too at the mention of Gab's name:

"Tell him we're expecting him one of these evenings, at the cave!"

The star up there, the star smiled with an emotional tenderness, which it expressed with a pearly ray of warmth…

On the way back, everyone meditated on these fabulous events. Only Raphaela sang, making pirouettes, the charms of which she alone knew…

…

20. Thaïs the Doe

Impatient, the friends arrived early for the meeting.

Raphaela was in beautiful form:

Her elegantly smoothed tail, sparkling coat and well-combed whiskers:

"Let's get going!" she said radiantly.

They went deeper into the oak forest. After an hour's walk, they arrived at the foot of a deserted hill.

"We have to go around it," Raphaela indicated.

They stopped in front of tall undergrowth, countless brambles, a veritable natural wall. Raphaela whistled seven times. Then the wall rose to let them in, to close instantly behind them.

"We take this staircase, but be careful, it goes downhill steeply! Paolo, help Josiane!"

At the bottom of the stairs, Spiridonos was waiting, in front of a fortification carved into the rock.

"You, you're are not going anymore!" groaned Raphaela.

"I know you, what's happened?"

With his defeated face, his tangled beard and his eyes filled with tears, Spiridonos replied:

"Sorry, I'm shaken! Leaving you yesterday, I ran into two young hunters. They had murdered a doe and injured another, whom I knew well. Terrifying…

But come closer, I'll let you in!"

In his turn he whistled seven times, and the bulkhead of the rock, without the slightest noise, moved aside:

What a spectacle:

A huge cave, with dozens of galleries. Dwarfs went from one gallery to another. They weaved in and out of small houses, aligned on the sides of the main gallery. All visibly busy with a very specific mission.

"It's unbelievable!" whispered Paolo, grabbing Josiane's hand.

"Come!" said Spiridonos, and led them into the first little house, right in the centre of the cave:

"I will introduce you to Abba Barnabas!"

Abba Barnabas, seated on an armchair carved in oak wood, was a gathering of a thousand lights. From his golden green eyes, sweeter than honey, to his bushy, curly beard, like a cascade of pearls.

And his smile…

His smile which never ceased to soothe…

He took Raphaela in his old arms:

"We miss you, why don't you come more often?"

Raphaela stared at him seriously:

"You know, with Uriel, it wasn't that easy anymore! He had to be taught manners, so that he didn't become a tyrannical little emperor!"

She gave him a wry wink:

"Love and discipline! It was you who taught me that! But now that he's grown up, the three of us will come!"

She went back to huddling against Spiridonos:

"Abba Barnabas, can we do nothing for the doe? Is she here?"

"No, we couldn't transport her! She's in terrible pain, so..."

"I know ... Spiridonos is going to take the potion to her!"

Spiridonos sobbed:

"Never seen so much rage for killing! I loved her so much! I saw her being born ..."

A dwarf, in a nurse's outfit, approached him and handed him a large bowl:

The potion…

"I'll leave you in the company of Abba Barnabas. I don't want to give up Spiridonos, I'm going with him!"

And as if it were part of a well-worn scenario, Raphaela followed Spiridonos to take Thaïs her last potion...

"We don't always manage to treat injured animals," sighed Abba Barnabas.

He gritted his teeth:

"Especially when they have been martyred by men!"

"With us," said Paolo, "when we hunt, it's for food."

"I cannot help myself," said Abba Barnabas, "I have to tell

you an Asian legend.

It is about Buddha.

At that time of his reincarnations, he was a gigantic deer in an Asian forest. He was the king of the deer tribe.

However, the prince who reigned over these territories, was a renowned hunter.

The great deer saw its tribe shrinking from year to year. He decided therefore to go and find the prince. He explained to him that soon, he would not even be able to hunt anymore, because the reserve was running low, and he suggested to him, that he limit his massacres.

He himself would send him, each new season, one of his subjects drawn at random.

Then they would have to wait for the next season. The prince agreed. The tribe could thus be preserved…

One day, the lot fell upon a young doe, who was raising her fawn.

At dawn, when the king saw the young faun crying, clinging to its mother, he could not bear the suffering:

"Stay here, close to your child! It's me, who will take your place!"

He named his successor and said goodbye to his family…

His head crowned with magnificent horns, like an imperial tiara, he advanced peaceful and determined. In the distance, he heard the dogs baying …

Suddenly, he found himself facing the prince, lance in hand, ready to kill:

"What are you doing here, King of the deer?" cried the

surprised prince.

The great deer told him, why he had sacrificed himself. The prince was so touched, that his heart opened. And he promised the great deer, that they would no longer hunt on his territories!

This is how, this forest has remained until today, a deer's paradise."

"Wonderful!" applauded Josiane. "I'll tell this story to my child!"

"And to all who entrust their hearts to you, to hear it…

But, my friends, it's high time that I show you around the cave…"

. . .

21. Life in the Cave

The little houses that surround the main gallery are our private residences. Here, we find ourselves in the main square, our daily meeting place.

We have a few simple health rules for the body and the soul:

Avoid pointless noise.

Take part every day in the mountain walks and bathing in the streams."

"And nobody bothers you?" asked John.

Abba Barnabas burst out laughing:

"But ... no one can see us! Josiane is one of the rare exceptions!

If someone sees us, the veil over their eyes has been lifted, so they can only be benevolent!

I continue:

Every evening, we meet, to discuss the problems of the day.

According to the motto of our elder:

"Problems are there to be solved!"[14]

We always strive to reconcile opposing opinions, without falling into the trap of being lukewarm about life.

Every morning we start the day with songs.

And everyone is reminded to smile. Smile at the other...

But what unites us most, is our work:

Each child is trained according to his gifts. With the possibility at any time, of retraining, provided you give the best of yourself. We combine a tough work ethic, with an intense awareness of the artistic life, as well as a respect for a wide variety of entertainment. To that end, we have a motley team of teachers, which allows our young people to get in touch very early, with the diversity of personalities."

"Are there also exams?" Paulo wanted to know.

"Of course! Again, in faithfulness to another of our elder's sayings:

"No matter what we do, we have to do it with our full commitment!"[15]

There are failures too.

But the foundation of our education is based on..."

He hesitated:

"I'm going to shock you, in your world, where success is taken so far into obsession, that no one left takes any chances. Here, our foundation, without seeking or provoking it,

---

[14] A motto repeated ceaselessly by our boarding school's headteacher, Dr Dietmar Pfister.
[15] Ibid. 14

which would be a blasphemous deviation, is:

The blessing of failure!"[16]

The friends frowned.

"Yes, we learn from an early age to deal with life's setbacks and debacles, that will inevitably cross each of our paths. By teaching ourselves the confidence, that every defeat, will be a source of renewal."

"There is always, since I say it, since I affirm it, at the end of sorrow an open window…"[17] recited John.

"Bravo!" replied Abba Barnabas.

"With us, failure does not exist! There are only new chances!

"With suffering or trauma, it's more complicated. Our team of psychologists is always present too."

His face lit up:

"Now, let's turn to our primary mission:

The restoration of the forest, but above all the protection of its weakest inhabitants:

We treat, as soon as we can, every injured animal. Come this way!"

Abba Barnabas led them to the entrance to the animal hospital.

Dwarfs carried stretchers, on which were lying hares, fawns, hinds, foxes, birds, hedgehogs…

And on tiny stretchers, caterpillars, bees, butterflies …

---

[16] Taken from the Good Friday homily, of my friend, Pater Andreas Agathokleous from Larnaka.
[17] Op. Cit. 8

"Our doctors and nurses are involved day and night."

"My frog?" cried Paolo.

"Your frog was bitten by a pike. It's the fourth time, it's been here, so fearless, this one!" Laughed Abba Barnabas.

"And what is it, that subtle scent that's embalming the whole cave?" asked Josiane.

"Here we are! Follow me!"

Abba Barnabas led the friends into a small cave. After raising a purple curtain of embroidered velvet, they entered a sort of sanctuary:

A dwarf was busy powering a big oil lamp, glimmering in front of an enormous portrait:

That of a lovely lady, all dressed in red. She had abundant hair, made up of thousands of small jasmine flowers. And the miracle was, that the flowers were alive! It was those that were exhaling that indescribable and intoxicating scent. In front of the lady, two other dwarfs were on their knees, their hands raised and their eyes full of reverence.

"What a beauty!" exclaimed Josiane.

"But the flowers? Do you water them?"

"Do you mean her hair? No. She…

She left them with us, upon departing."

"Abba, Abba, tell us!" Josiane begged.

Abba Barnabas, tugged at his long beard:

"I… not me! This story must be told…"

He pouted mischievously:

"By my wife, Anastasia."

Then, he whispered, as if he were telling a secret:

"It was she who met the Lady in red..."

...

22. The Lady in Red

Anastasia!" called Abba Barnabas. "Come see our friends!"

Anastasia came out of the house. Dressed all in light blue and white lace. She walked upright, but very slowly. Her face was a firework of silver wrinkles. She wore little round glasses, that were blue too.

She bowed:

"Very happy to meet you! It is not often that we have visitors."

"Led here by Raphaela!" added Abba Barnabas.

"Darling, our friends would like to know the story of the Lady in red!"

"Oh... in that case I'll sit down!"

She sat down. Her two chubby hands on her apron.

She didn't say a word, but just observed. Her eyes scrutinised each visitor, as if to make sure he or she was worthy, of hearing her story. She took her time, inclined her blue hat, crocheted with art:

"I do a lot of embroidery!"

She stopped:

"Besides, I was embroidering, when the tragedy happened..."

She joined her round, pink hands, pressing them to her heart:

"We did not have children and it saddened us. One day, however, although already old," she laughed:

"Yes, this was over 70 years ago!"

"You ... how old are you?" asked Paolo.

"Me 110, and Abba Barnabas 120."

"We live a long time," commented Abba Barnabas:

"We do not waste our energies. We eat little, and healthily. We sing, we dance a lot. We walk through the woods and above all, we all passionately love our work. But... Go on, my darling!"

"So, over 70 years ago, I got pregnant. We partied all night, and I gave birth to a beautiful boy."

She paused, for the time needed to take a loving look at Abba Barnabas:

"The complete image of his father! Bold, too! Barely on his feet, he was already starting to gallop everywhere! It was necessary at all costs, to take him with us into the woods. He often got lost, and it was the deer, who brought him back to us."

She took a long pause ...

"We were so happy, the three of us...

When he was seven years old, he announced that he would become a doctor, and God we were so proud…

One evening, coming back from school, he asked to go out and play. I was just embroidering and I let him, as usual. He…

Returning to the cave, he wanted to jump the stairs four at a time and …

He had a horrible fall. His head hit a step…"

Despite the years, one felt that this memory still tortured her.

"When they brought him back to me, it was too late. Blood was escaping from his head …"

Brave, she straightened hers, to show that she had withstood it:

"I thought I was going to die, too. I was in so much pain…

After the funeral, I no longer controlled my reactions. It was the first time that I didn't even listen to Abba Barnabas anymore.

It was winter, a Siberian winter.

I put on my cape, and ran away into the freezing night, screaming …

I was screaming out the name of my Nicolas! I wandered, rambling, as far as the hill. Despite the exhaustion, I started climbing like a wild thing, still screaming.

My hair was stuck together, like a mass of ice. Even my tears, had turned into ice cubes.

The night, however, was magical.

I'd never seen so many stars in the black sky…

When I got to the highest point on the hill, I collapsed in the snow. And I decided to wait for the cold to take me away, to join my beloved son…

I was already quite numb. The rip in my heart petrified in the ice, easing my suffering. Little by little, a veil slid over my eyes and I realised that I was going to leave too …

Suddenly, I was torn from my sweet agony, by a sparkling beam that was pouring out flames. Flames that did not burn, but enveloped with unfathomable tenderness. I thought I was dying and rejoiced in this heavenly state…

It was then that, at my feet, appeared…

The Lady in red.

Never, never had my eyes beheld something so immensely beautiful:

The sublime in its pure state:

Her red dress, like a vast shimmering cape, swirled in the wind. It looked like a volcano, with almost blinding colours. Her face was …

Just perfect. She blazed tenderness, intelligence and communion at the same time. And her hair! My friends, myriads of small jasmines, with a scent more intense than all of those you could gather together on Earth.

The Queen in red held out her hand to me:

"Come Anastasia, come!"

She took me to the highest peak in the Alps. All the stars stretched out their arms, to caress us gently, with bewitching warmth. I no longer knew, if I was dreaming, if I was dead…

If I was in heaven?

The Queen in red then took me in her arms:

"Take a good look, Anastasia:

I'll show you, what has become of your little Nicolas!"

And with a gesture of her dazzling hand, the stars all lined up, one facing the other. They bowed in reverence, and the ebony sky opened obediently:

It was at that moment that ..."

She stopped, her eyes too had become, two stars in front of a spectacle, eternally comforting.

"At that moment, I saw my little Nicolas, surrounded by six angels, who were lifting him up, teaching him to sing and dance. They accompanied him to the edge of the veil, facing the diamond lights, and my Nicolas called to me:

"Mummy, Mummy! You see how good I am here?

Don't cry anymore, darling Mother! One day, we will all be together again!

Don't cry anymore, my love! Mummy... it's me who'll protect you now!"

He was laughing my friends, he was laughing! He had never laughed like that!

Then he turned back round in the middle of the angels, and I saw on his back, that two small wings were pushing through. I questioned the Lady in red:

"Where are they going?"

"To my Son ...

The King of the universe and the Source of Life!"

A joy flooded with peace, then invited itself into my heart.

It has never left me...

When the last stars were returned to their places, I finally realised that my poor Abba Barnabas, must have been worried to death about it. Guessing my concern, the Queen in red took me in her arms:

"Yes, it is high time to return to the cave!"

Arriving at the cave, after having crossed clouds, hills, woods, and even the rock walls, I ran into Abba Barnabas' arms, to ask his forgiveness. In the middle of the night, he was the only one who was still awake. But the cave was invaded by a light so radiant, that dwarfs emerged from their sleep and one by one, they began to come out of their little houses.

"My friends, I bring Anastasia back to you!

And then… I wanted to visit you for a long time. Every day, I admire your courage and your kindness. So, I'm going to stay for a while! I'll teach you recipes, for potions to care for your animals. I will teach your children new poems, so that they grow, by refining their discernment. And to you, sacred songs, because my little angels, the words contain fabulous energies."

That's how the Lady in red came to stay with us for many months…

Abba Lukas, who has now joined our little Nicolas, had asked permission to paint her. Not only did the Queen in red accept, but it was she, who had us set up the sacred cave, where her portrait is located.

When Abba Lukas had finished, she congratulated him,

and offered us the gold lamp, which you could admire.

Alas, she had to leave. The day before her trip, she donated her jasmine hair to us."

Anastasia began to laugh:

"The funniest thing is that, without knowing that she was going to give us her hair, I had embroidered a veil for her, all in golden thread."

She added elegantly:

"Besides, she still wears it!

On the day of departure, we were all in the main square. The Queen in red with my gold veil on her head, was holding a magnificent box of pearls. It contained dozens of medallions, shaped like red hearts:

"My little guardian angels in the woods, I will offer each of you, a diamond chain with a red heart. On this heart is engraved a unique sentence, which will accompany you on your journey. It will also be a reminder, that I am watching over you!"

Then she passed through the walls again, in the same way she had entered..."

Anastasia half-opened her blouse and pulled out her red heart.

"What does it say?" asked Paolo, intrigued.

"It says:

Remember!"

The friends' eyes were filled with tears:

"Abba Barnabas, can we go back to the sacred cave?"

"Of course! And when you come back here, Anastasia will

prepare a good hot chocolate for you!"

...

It was with fear ...

One of those rare sacred fears, that the friends sat down, in front of the Queen in red...

They remained thus, each with his own story, his own pleas...

Then Paolo got up. He staggered a little. He walked over to the scented portrait:

He knelt down, and without even realising that he was speaking aloud, he addressed himself to the Queen in red:

"I beg you, show me the way too ...

The way, to work out what the best me is!"

He hesitated:

"If you can even find the best in me?"

He put his forehead on the ground:

"I beg you, give me...

Give me a red heart too!

A heart...

A pure heart..."

...

23. Raphaela

On leaving the sacred cave, Josiane kissed Paolo:
"Your face is bright!"

She stayed against him for a few moments, time for that rascal Agapi to spot them. She instantly drew out her arrows, sharpened like wisps. She aimed right on target! They didn't even notice. They simply looked at each other, like never before ...

When they got back to Abba Barnabas', Anastasia looked at them inquisitively. She did not say a word, but rejoiced:

"Agapi has had her way again! So much the better, these two really need it!"

The very moment, that they took their places, Raphaela and Spiridonos entered. Raphaela looked ruffled, half buried in the beard of Spiridonos, who had rediscovered his serene smile:

"Thaïs left without suffering. She even recognised Raphaela, who was a great support to me!"

"We'd drink a chocolate, too!" begged Raphaela.

"So my darlings, you don't regret coming?"

"Raphaela, what a gift you gave us, by bringing us here!"

Raphaela shook the twigs off her coat:

"My treasures, you have contributed to it! Let's also extend recognition to our Josiane, whose distress has been overcome!"

She waggled her whiskers:

"What a snub to tribulation! You know what Gab always says:

"Never give up!""

"How is it," asked Paolo, "that you know this magical place?"

Raphaela burst out with her prettiest laugh:

"It's a long story!"

She winked mischievously at Spiridonos:

"A very long story ..."

"Raphaela, tell it!" pleaded John, who had just handed Tatiana over to the Queen in red. "Okay, but Spiridonos must tell his share, too!"

She climbed back into his lap, gripping the curls of his beard, which made everyone laugh:

"In fact, I was born in this forest.

In the big oak tree, under which we had our meetings. The year I was born, it got cold very early. It snowed much earlier than usual. Mum had to go out often, looking for food. I was rather frail. She wanted to get stronger, so that I could get good milk.

One morning she left, as usual. She never came back…

I waited for her, shivering. All day…

When evening came, distraught, I started to cry. I felt so alone, so lost. I ventured outside the nest, shouting:

"Mummy, Mummy, come back!"

I fell.

A long fall. My body was in pieces, and I passed out…

Continue godfather, it's your turn!"

Spiridonos, his eyes overflowing with affection, caressed her head:

"I was going back to the cave, after an exhausting day. But an inner voice made me go back to the forest. I found her under the oak. At first I thought she was dead. But she was breathing. So, I wrapped her in my beard," he lit up cheerfully:

"That's why she likes to go back there so much!

When I got to the cave, I rushed to our hospital. However, the surgeons and the doctors explained to me, that there was nothing more to be done, except to brew the potion…

I begged them to try, and stayed close to her at each operation. I watched over her day and night, while the dwarfs took turns with the Lady in red, so that the miracle could take place…

The most beautiful moment of my life, was when she opened her eyes!

I bottle-fed her. She healed and became this beautiful cherub…

Normally, she should have stayed in our convalescent

ward. But, as she was so young, I received permission from Abba Lukas, to keep her at my house."

"He taught me everything!" Raphaela couldn't help adding.

Spiridonos had trouble concealing his emotion:

"God she was brave and determined!

She integrated perfectly into the life of the cave and even became a competent auxiliary nurse.

I knew, however, that her life was not here. We all knew it!

One day, Abba Lukas explained to us, that the time had come give her back her freedom.

The problem was, she didn't know anyone in the forest, and we didn't want to lose her. So we decided to wait for Gab's next visit..."

He paused and the two exchanged colluding winks.

"My friends, if you had seen Gab! No sooner had they presented her to him, than he stopped moving, as if struck by thunder."

"It was mainly lightning that hit him, and dwarf Agapi really needn't have involved herself!" Anastasia hastened to comment.

Spiridonos nodded:

"So she left with Gab ..."

Raphaela stood up gracefully:

"But he didn't court me right away! He was too respectful of my freedom! He led me to his kingdom and introduced me to all the squirrels. They offered me a little nook on a big fir tree and taught me my new life."

She reprised the prolonged game with her eyelashes:

"I was very, very pretty! All the gentlemen were courting me, including the beautiful black one."

Her eyes seemed intoxicated by a beautiful memory:

"I chose Gab, and we got married! What's more, we got married here, in the cave. Godfather was my witness, and Anastasia was Gab's."

"Raphaela, why do you call Spiridonos, Godfather?" Josiane wanted to know.

"Because," Spiridonos replied in a flash, "it was I who chose her name for her!"

"And why did you call her Raphaela?" asked Paolo.

"Godfather, let me tell them!"

"Over to you my darling, over to you…"

Raphaela climbed onto a wooden stool. She looked prayerful, filled with desire…

She closed the little jewels of her eyes many times. She spread her arms, as if she was going to dance. She lifted them as high as she could, joining her adorable little hands together then proclaimed, very quietly:

"Because Raphaela means: God heals…"

…

The farewells turned into bursts of tenderness. Raphaela promised to come back with Gab and Uriel.

And the little troop set off again …

…

24. Doctor Georgy

A s they entered the seminar room, the next day, they were all on cloud nine...

"Hello everyone, let me introduce myself:

I am of Russian origin, a psychiatrist and Gab's friend.

I will do my best to be precise and concrete, to add my stone on the path to your liberation:

First of all, whatever the trauma, speak up!

Imagine you have 10, 20, 30, 40 kilograms or more, of mud stuck to your chest. You are suffocating! Even though this mud is old and starting to dry out.

Among the methods that I practice, there is EMDR[18].

---

[18] Discovered in 1987 by American psychologist, Francine Shapiro, (1948-2019) of the Mental Research Institute in Palo Alto, California, EMDR (Eye Movement Desensitization and Reprocessing) consists of have a trauma patient perform a series of eye movements to obtain neuro-emotional integration of traumatic memories left untreated by the brain so not integrated into the patient's experience who thereby suffers from flashbacks, panic attacks, nightmares etc.

Eye movement therapy, which will not erase traumatic shocks, but will make them less offensive.

I will now summarise some common-sense measures, so often overlooked unfortunately: Somatics first of all:

Get your body fully involved, it will be your best ally:

Good food.

Restorative sleep.

Sport, deep breathing, walking, massages, reflexology...

Psychological next:

When your head explodes, immediately refocus on the present moment! If possible, by performing an ordinary task.

Become the master of your awesome iPhone, not its slave!"

"Can you add a word on social media? John asked.

"A magnificent opportunity! But try to use it for authentic sharing! You're not robots, and neither are the ones you are connected with!

I continue:

Welcome work as real therapy!

And remember:

Your story, even the worst, can become a source of renewal! However, you have to know how to be patient, to sometimes let yourself be carried away...

And then my children, absolutely cultivate an ideal! There is one for each of you!"

Doctor Georgy paused for a long time. As if he wanted to give everyone, the chance to tap into the reserves of their emotions, their instincts, their dreams...

He resumed, weighing each of his words:

"Don't worry about mockery or failure, dare!

Explore every corner of your abilities, your gifts, your energies, to achieve your projects!" Gab and Raphaela couldn't help but exclaim together:

"And never give up!"

...

Josiane stood up:

"I have suffered...

Such traumatic abuse since my childhood...

Can psychotherapy and EMDR set me free?"

Doctor Georgy took his time ...

Gab had the good idea, of jumping onto her shoulder and stroking her hair.

"Of course, for these shocks that torture soul and body, I strongly recommend a form of psychotherapy:

Avoid replaying the same unconscious patterns throughout your life. Equally you can try the EMDR approach. But I permit myself to complete this advice:

There is a moment when, you have to force yourself to take a leap...

To reach forgiveness."

"How can you force yourself? John asked.

"Start with just one small second a day!" Dr Georgy smiled:

"Believers, name in your prayers whoever has hurt you.

Atheists, send him a thought of success and happiness!

My friends, healing does not begin when we merely

understand, but when we have been able to forgive! Experience it, you will see, that you will be the first to benefit!

This will be my conclusion! Do not be discouraged, I am not there myself! This is the crowning achievement of liberation, for all. In the meantime, I am at your disposal, for those who would like a personal interview ... "

"But first, we'll teach you a dance!" Gab laughed.

"One of the many dances of our cave friends!

Come my darling!"

The very beautiful, the very sweet one joined Gab on the desk:

"It is very simple!" Raphaela said, standing on her back legs, facing Gab:

"We take a step back, hands on hips. Then a step forward, and we join our hands to those of our partner, keeping our arms raised. Then we take four steps to the side, and start again." "Is that it?" laughed Paolo, the king of the dance!

"Wait Paolo, wait for the essentials:

However long the dance lasts, the rule is never to take your eyes off your partner's. It is called: "The dance of the eyes."

Music!"

The simplest thing happened. And as often is with the simplest things:

The most sublime thing:

Raphaela and Gab's eyes poured out an ocean of stars! Not only on each other, but also on all the friends, who then realised that no one else was watching...

The eyes!

A pure moment of paradise, as only Gab and Raphaela knew how to offer...

When the music ceased, Gab bowed to his sweetheart, and the friends understood, that even their awesome iPhone could never teach them how to perform such a loving bow...

"This afternoon, I will give a summary of our meetings."

He stopped himself…

Nobody wanted him to announce the rest …

"Our seminar is coming to an end. I am sad to leave you, but we remain united, invisibly."

"More than that!" Raphaela said happily, "there will be a very visible surprise reunion!"

She laughed, raising her adorable little snout:

"Right here!"

"She's running on ahead of herself, my darling! Truth is, I think she's so eager to see you again, that she's having trouble holding her tongue!"

During the meal, all were wondering what the surprise would be, and eager to return to the seminar room.

Little Uriel, who was wearing one of the CC T-shirts, with the beautiful portrait of his mum, and one of the CC caps[19] with his dad on, was already saying his goodbyes, receiving his overdose of hugs and candy …

. . .

---

[19] Both available at www.mariaandreas.eu

25. Gab's Closing Seminar

My friends, the path you have chosen at CordisClub, remains a conquest. You will have to accept the falls, the relapses, the crossings of the desert...

The doubt! Yes, no real path, without doubting!

No authenticity either, without accepting the diversity and uniqueness of everyone! Don't be afraid of differences, they will broaden your horizon. I really like this quote from the Malian writer and ethnologist, Amadou Hampâté Bâ, which our Paolo gave us:

"If you think like me, you are my brother. If you don't think like me, you are twice my brother, because you will open up another world to me."

However, to share and transmit, it's still necessary to be anchored in one's cultural, social or religious roots. Do not flout your own, under the pretext of an amalgamation of tolerances, which no longer mean anything.

May each Unique Person become once again rich in his or her uniqueness, therefore a fruitful member of the whole Body...

Support each other! With no other judgement than compassion! Together, spot harmful suggestions as quickly as possible, before they rule your hearts, or cause you to react uncontrollably.

There is, however, a danger: that of suffocating all vitality:

Also, practice turning the energies of destructive passions back into creative passions! A small, very concrete personal example:

I was jealous of the beautiful black one's coat! "

"Oh no again? Gab, my darling, you are the most beautiful one!"

"I know… but the passion of jealousy was there! SO I harnessed jealousy's energy!

I started doing sit-ups, eating better and looking for essential oils, to smooth my coat!"

Gab stood on his forepaws. He stepped forward in front of the swooning Raphaela.

The friends applauded, laughing…

"I continue:

Talking is a therapeutic key, but also a trap.

We can talk too much! Add stuff, consciously or unconsciously. Or, with the possible manipulation of a therapist, even talk about a "traumatic" event that was never experienced!"

"That's screwy?" Paolo exclaimed.

"How do we sort what's real?"

"Ask Mike, who knows you better than you do. He will know how to instil into you the sacred fear in front of the word. So that your story is closest to the truth, which accords with beauty. Personally, I believe that not even every truthful account strengthens the accusation. Never forget, the accuser is Beelzeb!

This is all very subtle and on a razor's edge, so I can't recommend enough, that you go to competent and well-trained people!" Gab sat up on his two back paws. He was watching his friends, with his Gab smile...

"Watch out for illusions! Do not try to imitate your idols! Rather, tap into the richness of your historical and cultural roots.

And above all my friends:

Patiently practice internalising that each trial, each failure, is a new chance!

I have a nice anecdote about a 4th century hermit, Macarius of Egypt:

After a life of battling demons, Macarius leaves this world.

Little by little his soul rises and ascends to heaven. Beelzeb, fought relentlessly by the saint, during his earthly life, approaches him taunting him:

"Bravo Macarius, you've reached your goal now!"

And the great ascetic replied:

"Not yet, not yet ..."

This will be my conclusion my beloveds:

Cultivate perseverance! Strive to be cheerful, not because

everything is going well, but because you have made your choice. It is Beelzeb who eggs you on towards misery, depression and passiveness, to manipulate you better in the drift. Also, I repeat it:

Never give up!"

Gab stretched out his two beautiful arms, once again, glowing with tenderness:

"Now?"

He started to leap from one table to another, flying about in agile pirouettes:

"I'll leave my Raphaela, to announce the surprise to you!"

Still as delicate and prettier than an angel:

"My darlings, see you here in October for..."

Mischievously she jumped on Paolo's shoulder:

"A wedding!"

"It's not true?" exclaimed John.

"They didn't tell me anything!"

Tender Raphaela, was more precise:

"The marriage of Paolo and Josiane."

Applause, tears, laughter and ...

Relief that Beelzeb had received a hell of a slap in the face!

"That's not all!" Paolo added proudly:

"After the birth of the child, Josiane gifted in drawing, will take online lessons. She hopes one day to work in marketing design.

As for me, I'm going to take a management training course, because I would like, to open my own workshop as a car mechanic!"

Raphaela clapped her hands, and she started her dance again. With her unique precision. Her languid and yearning rhythm, the mark of Raphaela's grace! Then she intoned melodiously this improvised refrain:

Look at your star,
Deep in the sky,
The one you love,
The one you lost,
They will be there!

Look at your star,
Deep in your heart,
The one you were,
The one you are.
And will become.

Look at your star,
Deep in your soul,
And take the way,
The one you choose,
To climb the hill!

Look at your star,
Deep in the sun,
There is courage,
To build your life,
To build your love!

Look at your star,
Deep in your light,

And you will find,
How to fight,
To work and win!

Look at your star,
Deep in your eyes,
Deep in our eyes,
And you will see,
The ones we are,
Becoming stars!

Gab regarded her, filled with a fiery love, and everyone was once again in awe of her, who was prettier than an angel...

Then Paolo took Josiane in his arms:

She cried. For the first time in her life, she was crying ...

Tears of happiness ...

...

Up there, much higher than the hostel, much higher than the Swiss Alps, much higher than the clouds ...

Mike was tilting his gold and diamond curls, with a smile of divine tenderness, for these two entwined creatures. And he sent them a little of his breath, to protect them ...

...

PART THREE

RETURNS

26. Goodbyes

Once again they were swimming, closer in friendship than ever.

It was John, who was the first to whisper:

"To think, I owe all this to Tatiana!"

"And to your grandpa's prayers, John, don't forget him!"

"You're right Paolo! I am so happy to be telling him about my pilgrimage to the Holy Mountain. "

"You weren't made to be a monk John, I know you, but go for it! Except this time, I can't go with you!"

As they left, they were shivering, but they felt such inner heat, that their teeth forgot to chatter…

…

The suitcases were ready.

In front of the house, each of them wearing a CC T-shirt[20], the friends were waiting for the squirrel family.

---

[20] Available on the website www.mariaandreas.eu

Suddenly, one of those sublime imperial eagles, began to spin in the sky, making big circles above their heads.

A splendour.

"Gab," Paolo called, "come and see this marvellous wonder in the heavens!"

Gab came out and burst out laughing:

"Our plane!"

The splendour settled itself at the top of the stairs. The friends held their breath…

Gab, Raphaela and little Uriel climbed on the back of the majestic bird:

"Thank you Johannis, we're going home! See you very soon my lifelong friends, friends of our hearts!"

They stood there as if in a dream, until Johannis and the little family had disappeared behind the clouds…

Then, John finished loading the car, while Paolo and Josiane got into the back.

The journey seemed short to them. Nobody spoke as each was trying to hoard away for the future the intense memories of this magical week…

…

When he arrived home, John kissed his parents, his little brother and immediately went to the retirement home:

"My little one! My Johnny!"

John was back in his favourite position.

Kneeling at the feet of the giant of light…

"Grandpa, I'm coming to ask …"

He was searching for his words:

"I come to ask for your blessing, I...

I'm going to leave for the Holy Mountain!"

The angel of silence instantly slipped into the room.

They remained thus without moving. Again, John had buried his hands in those of his grandpa, that were so wrinkled yet so soft…

A silver tear then began to flow, uninterrupted, over the old man's cheek:

"Glory to God!" were the only words, he could manage to utter in his emotion…

…

27. The Holy Mountain

Here, you are well and truly stuffing yourself on the divine!" John smiled, in sending this message to his friend. He added to himself: "And you throw all your own shit up!" But he didn't write it down.

It was two months, since he was welcomed into one of the most famous monasteries on Mount Athos. He had imagined a peaceful retreat. A bit like a holiday of the soul...

What an earthquake!

The only hours of respite were those in the chapel, for the long offices.[21] John didn't understand a word, but he struggled patiently, trying not to be overwhelmed by his thoughts. He either absorbed the songs of the monks intuitively, or he immersed himself in the grandiose frescoes. From day one, he had experienced appeasement through the

---

[21] Chapel services

magnificence of the paintings, that covered the walls and ceiling of the church.

The rest of the time, he peeled the vegetables for the multitude of pilgrims, while talking to a hieromonk from England. He explained to him that in fact, although he'd been baptised Orthodox, he did not have the faith. He just promised Christ, to come here, if He healed a loved one.

"The paths are unique for each of us!" replied the hieromonk.

"But what do I do with mine? How do I take one more step?"

"The breath of our life at La Sainte Montagne, is in this prayer, which we repeat as often as possible:

"Lord Jesus Christ, Son of God, have pity on me!""

John heard the message, but he didn't really want to start the prayer ...

His nights were appalling. He was capsized by his memories, which were blown up, like hundreds of disfigured and grimacing gnomes.

Orgies.

Drugs.

Drinking sessions…

But also, the caresses and softness of Tatiana's body. Her smile that he missed so much.

Her sudden departure for Japan…

Every night, Jimmy's coffin, immense, passed through…

He had come to seek peace, he met with war!

Also, it was with daily relief that he heard the monastery

bell ring at 3:00am, for offices.

He always jumped from his soiled pilgrim's bed. Soiled from sweat. From furtive, tasteless releases...

Often, the beginning of the liturgy coincided with the sublime sunrise over the sea.

Then...

John realised that all this had a meaning.

A link.

A union.

A communion....

...

One day, he decided to pursue his pilgrimage...

He wanted to climb the Holy Mountain's highest summit. He took his leave of the monks and he set off, under the sun of fire...

...

28. The Ascent

Once again, John was climbing.

Solitarily.

As far as the eye could see, the olive trees, the pines and the burnt scrub.

John was completely alone.

Very quickly, his prayer was thwarted by multiple voices. Voices who told him his own words. His many lies. His betrayals. His resentments. His scorn for Josiane when she was pleasuring him...

He also saw himself, cursing Tatiana, for succumbing to the call of her mutilated heart. He remembered his rage, to crush the Japanese guy, his instant escape into vodka...

The sun was slapping him ruthlessly, but he quickened his pace, to sweat more. As if to wash himself with the oozings of his hideous memories...

And suddenly:

The miracle of the Holy Mountain was accomplished:

John collapsed on the parched grass and burst into tears...

Finally, he could cry. To spit out in his tears, all the grime of his heart:

John was crying as he had never cried. Not even, after Jimmy's death.

A few yards away from him, he saw a big viper. It was sliding along the rocky path. He watched it retreat, noiselessly. Harmoniously languorous...

Smiling from this symbolic wink, he welcomed then...

Nature:

The beauty of the mountain, the skites, the monasteries scattered in front of the queen, the queen in dark blue, infinite...

He wanted to run down again, to dive into her. But he took out his cakes and his dried fruit, and after a frugal meal, he fell asleep under a pine tree. Remembering Gab's words:

"Tears of sincere regret, are the deliverance of the soul!"

He felt washed clean.

Wrung out...

He ended by falling asleep, in a state of peacefulness unknown until then...

...

...

29. The Old Standing Giant

When he awoke, the furnace had softened. A sea breeze brushed the mountain. John stood up. He started walking again. And for the first time in his life, he recited the prayer:

"Lord Jesus Christ, Son of God, have pity on me ..."

He was climbing now with an unlocked agility...

Towards evening, he crossed a small wood with its intense odours, and became drunk on the singing of birds. Arriving at the wood's exit, he saw a strange form in the distance. A kind of human:

A giant, with a human appearance...

John stopped, surprised and curious. The colossus was approaching...

His curved back, with an old canvas bag, filled with plants and roots.

When the giant hermit got to his height, John wondered, if he was straight from antiquity.

So tattered were his clothes, his skeletal legs, his tangled hair. His long beard, cluttered with twigs and the remains of wild berries, seemed to spring from a past universe.

The hermit bowed and motioned for him to follow him...

The evening sweetness embraced them with affection. The emperor of heaven began his descent on the violet horizon, with its orange streaks. The accomplishment of beauty. The Beauty of creation!

John slowed down, taking his pace from the old hermit…

They arrived at a kind of cave with a wooden door, at least a hundred years old.

The hermit pushed the door open, and let John entered first:

It was in this big hole, that the hermit lived:

Some old icons, a lit nightlight, a cross, a single stool and...

A form of ...

Of bed? A tomb rather, carved in stone.

John realised that, when the hermit took a little rest, he took it in his future tomb…

On the stone, a faded but still very visible fresco, representing the Dormition of the Mother of God[22].

John then recognised:

The Lady in red, radiant with peace...

Near her body, her Son standing, come to seek her soul, represented by a baby swaddled in bands. John couldn't take his eyes off the fresco, as the hermit sorted through his herbs and roots...

---

[22] Celebrated by Orthodox Christians on 15th August

It was at that moment, on this lost mountain, at the bottom of this cave, opposite the future tomb of his host, that John experienced his first reconciliation with death:

Before the sleeping Mother of God!

So beautiful.

So… dead and still so alive…

And he felt overwhelmed by a strange desire:

That of stopping there. To lie down in the bed of stone, and to wait in his turn, for the King of the universe to come to seek his soul …

The hermit snapped him out of his reverie, offering him fresh figs. Night had enveloped the cave. Through the window, you could see the stars, immense. So immense and so close.

The old giant motioned for John to sit on the stool, but John tried to sign, that it was up to him to sit down! The old hermit shook his head, pointing his finger at the icons and the nightlight. Then he planted himself in front of his small altar of prayers and began to sing his offices.

John sat down. He waited…

An expectation that turned into a journey:

A journey to the depths of the night. To the depths of the centuries. To the depths of those prayers, recited thousands of times, by monks, hermits, pilgrims.

A journey too, to the depth of his heart …

At times the hermit chanted, at times he sang, then prostrated himself.

He got up. Knelt. He seemed to beg. Tirelessly…

The hours passed, without passing. Time ... time was slipping away ...

Into the other time.

The time before.

The time of always.

The new time...

In the middle of the night, John fell asleep on the wooden stool, lulled by the therapeutic whisper of the hermit's prayers...

...

When one of the first rays of light entered the cave, John opened his eyes:

The old giant was finishing his services. Then he went out, still without saying a word, and brought back some figs. He handed them to John, his eyes darker than the night and brighter than the sun.

Never, had John contemplated such beautiful eyes:

So big. So flamboyant. So overflowing with Love...

The hermit put his canvas bag back on his shoulders, and walked out of the cave:

He sat. He finally sat down! On an archaic bench in front of the entrance...

John joined him, as in a dream:

Side by side, tasting juicy figs, in the eternity of the present, facing the standing star. Opposite the blue queen...

When the old giant stood up, John returned to get his bag. He bowed to the hermit, with both hands outstretched, to receive the benediction:

Then…

The old giant stood up, put his big rough, scratched hand on John's head and whispered: "The woman…

The woman with the slanted eyes:

She is waiting for you!

It's her, who needs you now!"

Then, he took the same path, from where he had come the day before …

...

30. Thank You!

John was shaking.

From head to toe.

He was shaking with exhaustion. He was shaking with wonder. He was shaking with joy! From this renewed joy, that oozes forgiveness and purified love.

But also…

From that pure joy of being in love!

The descent turned into a tumble…

For one more time, John was running down the mountain.

But that morning there, under the flame of the complicit sun. He quickly jumped on the first boat towards the port of Ouranoupoli. Literally: the city of heaven. It is there that the orthodox pilgrim wives wait for their husbands, on their return from the Holy Mountain…

He was not even surprised, to see a ridiculous hat in the distance.

A pink canvas hat.

The only hat he hoped for:

She was waiting for him …

The woman.

The woman with slanting eyes:

His Tatiana was waiting for him.

…

He descended first.

She did not move.

Frozen.

Beneath her tears.

Beneath that dazzling blaze.

Beneath her ridiculous pink hat...

He savoured the few seconds that separated him from her. A few seconds more:

Just time to whisper:

"Thank you my God!

Thank you…"

…

Up there, much higher than the little harbour, much higher than the blue queen, much higher than the star of fire...

Mike was tilting his gold and diamond curls, with a smile of divine tenderness, for these two entwined creatures. And he sent them a little of his breath, to refresh them...

———————————

The End.
Bienne, October 28th 2020, the festival of the Protection of the Lady in red.

The Author

Born in Algeria, with Swiss/French dual-nationality, Maria Andreas sat her baccalaureate at La Chaux-de-Fonds, in French-speaking Switzerland. She then travelled for two years across Asia and Africa in a campervan. After studying modern languages (Zürich, Cambridge), she worked for 25 years as a French teacher in German-speaking Switzerland. Then she moved to Bordeaux and resumed studies in orthodox theology (Paris) and applied psychology (Düsseldorf). During this time she engaged in a long analysis with Professor Gérard Ostermann, in Bordeaux. During a one-year stay in Cyprus, she fell in love with the Greek language and the spirituality of Orthodox monasteries. It was then that she returned to her writing which, as a high school student, had already earned her first prize in Strasbourg's 1967 European Essay competition.

www.mariaandreas.eu

OTHER BOOKS BY
MARIA ANDREAS

Der Tod hat keine Augen - Paramon, 2005
La Mort n'a pas Dieu - Amazon, 2017
Intenses - Amazon, 2017
La Maladie, Mon Ennemie Complice - Amazon, 2018
Illness, My Complicit Enemy - Amazon, 2018
Arthrose, Ostéoporose, Cancer du Sein et Autres Fléaux - Amazon, 2019
Arthritis, Ostéoporosis, Breast cancer and Other Scourges - Amazon, 2019
La Dixième Plaie - Amazon, 2020
Sparkles of Intensity - Amazon, 2020
Die Krankheit, Mein Komplizenhafter Feind - Amazon, 2020
The Tenth Plague – Huge Jam, 2021

Printed in Great Britain
by Amazon